The Downfall

John Hagen

Dedication

To Ileana, my wife, who remains my voice of reason and the source of my happiness.

Acknowledgment

Over 40 years as a surgeon, I've seen colleagues plummet from their high positions, their downfall a stark and cautionary tale. The medical field demands a level of precision, ethical behavior, and dedication far exceeding what's typically expected from most professions. Throughout the majority of my life, I have been incredibly fortunate to have the distinct privilege of serving as a surgeon, providing care for my patients; however, the contemplation of how an individual might successfully navigate and overcome the profound and devastating effects of a professional crisis that significantly impacts their personal life has consistently captivated my interest while also causing me considerable concern.

It is important to note that this novel is a work of fiction, and any resemblance to actual persons, living or dead, is purely coincidental. I take full responsibility and acknowledge that any and all errors found within the manuscript are my sole fault and oversight.

I would like to take this opportunity to express my deepest gratitude to Janet Gyenes for her invaluable contributions, including her meticulous editing and insightful suggestions, which significantly enhanced the quality of the final product. I wish to express my sincere gratitude to Dr. Bev Adams for generously donating her time to review and meticulously correct some of the psychiatric information I had. I want to express my heartfelt thanks to the incredibly dedicated team at KDP Publishing, whose collective hard work and unwavering commitment have been instrumental in the successful completion and publication of this novel.

About The Author

Dr. John Hagen completed his doctor of medicine (honours) degree from the University of Alberta in 1979, later attaining specialty training in areas such as endoscopy. He's spent much of his practice in Toronto-area hospitals in roles such as attending surgeon, division head of general surgery, surgical director of bariatrics, and chief of surgery, chief of staff, among others. Now retired from practice, Hagen has taken on several instructor responsibilities: he currently holds a trio of roles as supervising surgeon and instructor at the University of Toronto Surgery Training Program, and has won several teaching awards for his work. Since 2005, Hagen has lectured widely and delivered myriad courses and live demonstrations, particularly in laparoscopic and bariatric surgery, in Canada, the US, UK, Europe, Mexico, Nepal, Colombia and China.

The Downfall is Hagen's seventh novel, following six other medical thrillers, *The Heir*, 2024, *The Clinic*, 2024, *The Embryo* (2023), *The Mission* (2024), *The Complication* (2024) and *The Sailor* (2023). Along with being a dedicated lecturer and volunteer at medical missions with his wife, Ileana, the couple are avid travellers and sailors. They live in King City, Ontario, and spend time taking excursions on their 51-foot sailboat, *Ileana,* having sailed to the Caribbean and the Bahamas for the winter months. Read about his sailing adventures on www.dreamingofileana.com

Contents

Prologue

With the cold, imposing structure of the hospital looming behind him, Carl pushed himself to run faster, the weight of his anxiety pressing down on him. Sweat drenched his body, his heart hammering against his ribs, a frantic rhythm against the silence. He could feel his pace quickening, and each breath a desperate gasp for air. Another wave of anxiety washed over him, a burning reminder of the sharp, stabbing pain in his abdomen that worsened with every stride. The cold, impersonal hospital sped past him; the source of his problems. He knew he had to get away. Aware of the risk of intense physical exertion causing a heart attack from an over exercised stressed heart, he craved that end. He imagined that would finally ease the relentless, free-floating anxiety that had been a dark companion for the past three months, a constant hum of unease in the background of his life.

The hope he clung to, a fragile thing like a bug about to fly into a windshield, was that one day his life would return as it had been before his downfall. He wished he could restore his happy life, lifting the weight of his mistake from his shoulders and filling his senses with the sweetness of freedom. Picturing the sun on his face and the wind in his hair, he sailed across Lake Ontario with his wife, Andrea, and his children, Carl Junior, and Simone. He could see them laughing, their joyous cries echoing across the water as the boat gently rocked on the waves and imagined a feeling of peace and contentment washing over him as he gripped the wheel.

Carl looked at his watch; the faint glow of the digital display read 2:15 a.m., the silence of the night pressing in on him. For his 32nd birthday, Andrea gifted him a heavy, beautifully crafted Breitling Navitimer self-winding watch; its cool metal casing felt substantial on his wrist. The value of it was $6000. The pawn shop offered him $1000 cash for his cherished possession, but the memories it held were too precious to trade for money.

His rapid pace finally caught up to him, his breath coming in ragged gasps, and he stopped running, his legs trembling, feeling like he was about to faint. A harsh, whistling wheeze escaped his lips as he landed heavily on the ground, his head thrown back to the inky blackness of the star-filled sky, desperate to stay upright. His ragged breathing eased as the realization dawned that his attempt to induce a heart attack, a desperate bid to end his misery, had failed.

Chapter 1

The applause was thunderous. Dr. Carl Mackenzie looked at the 450 surgeons from across Ontario, who had taken two days off from their busy schedule to come to his meeting. A hush fell over the conference hall as Carl scanned the room, noticing the expectant smiles on the faces of the attendees. With his six-foot-two-inch frame, sharp angles to his jaw and cheekbones, his quiet intensity commanded attention; the air around him crackled with unspoken power. Carl's fine facial features and intense blue eyes stared out from the posters, the image crisp and sharp, promising an electrifying meeting. His short brown hair, stylish salt-and-pepper beard, and trim suit made him look like he belonged in a QC magazine spread.

"Thank you, thank you," he said into the microphone as his confident voice boomed through the loudspeakers, echoing off the walls. "I am honoured to be elected as your president to the Surgical Society. Thank you for placing your trust in me. I will wait until noon to deliver the bulk of my presidential address, but I have exciting news that I cannot keep to myself any longer. The bargaining team has negotiated a 9.5% increase in our surgical fees each year for the next three years. This will be retroactive to April 1st."

The room broke into a thunderous applause with hooting and

cheers from the surgeons. Carl knew that this would be a great way to start his term as president. Nobody in the room, including himself, was expecting such a generous increase. He held up his hand and the room became quiet. "With the widespread shortage of doctors across the country, the government has made a concerted effort to attract and retain talented medical staff, specifically surgeons, to prevent us from seeking more lucrative opportunities in the United States. This made it easier for us to get the increase in fees that had fallen behind the rate of inflation for the past five years. The new government has promised me they would improve the quality of service in the health care system under their leadership." All the delegates stood up and broke into another round of applause with more hooting and cheers.

The outstanding financial update provided to him by the bargaining team left no room for doubt that the rest of the meeting would unfold as a resounding success. Carl held up his right hand and the noise settled. Some continued to whisper to each other. "We have a terrific program today with talks from some of you that are truly world class. I'll hand off to the program director, Dr. Rob Maclean." A quiet applause followed, and Dr. MacLean took to the podium.

"That was quite the surprise!" said a voice whispered into his ear as Carl walked off the stage. It was his surgical partner, Sebastian Rhodes.

"It was a surprise for me as well," said Carl. "The Minister of Health, Aaron Cohen, asked me to come to his office last week for a meeting. He said he wanted to correct the adversarial approach of the previous government and asked what it would take to do this. I kick myself for not asking for more, though. I think it was a missed opportunity."

"Ha ha," laughed Sebastian. "And everyone in the crowd thinks you bargained hard and fiercely for achieving the settlement!"

Carl smiled and pointed his finger in a friendly manner at Sebastian. "Don't you go dispel my God like image with them. Since these moments occur so rarely in one's life, I kindly ask to be allowed to relish in my 15 minutes of fame."

"Don't you worry about that. I plan to ride the wave with you. Our small-town practice in Guelph is now on the map thanks to you. Our surgical practice is booming since the news of you becoming president hit the local papers. We have never had it so good. The hospital administrators are bending over backwards to upgrade our laparoscopic equipment to match the increase in demand from our practice. The new surgical robot will be here next week. This is the best thing that has happened to me as a surgeon in 15 years at the hospital."

"Let's go with the flow." Carl's face became serious as he

pondered. "It won't always be this way, so we have to milk my celebrity status for every cent while it lasts."

"Why so serious? You are a star! Your patients love you. They think you walk on water. The admin loves your low complication rates and the positive reviews on social media. What is there not to like? With your superb surgical skills and your radiant personality, your 15 minutes of fame will last for years."

Carl broke into a wide smile. "You are so kind. Thank you." Carl patted his partner on the back. "I had better go check with registration to see if there are any issues that I don't know about."

Carl walked to the registration desk and looked at the tally of delegates. They had budgeted for 390 participants. With a few last-minute walk-ins, they expected 410 surgeons. 450 had turned up. "Oh oh," said Carl to Marlene, the registration clerk. "We are going to have a problem with the lunch. There are too many attendees here."

"I've taken care of it," said Marlene. "I had a conversation with the caterers a few minutes ago and they have agreed to increase the number for lunch. Attendees can also look forward to an increased supply of coffee and pastries during the designated break times."

"You are amazing, Marlene!" exclaimed Carl. "We have another successful meeting, thanks to you." Carl saw Marlene blush slightly as she waved her hand as if to say it was all part of the job.

"The success is all because of you," said Marlene. Her eyes shone bright blue as she stared at him. "You are the one that is amazing."

Carl walked away with an empty feeling in the pit of his stomach. His psychiatrist, Raymond Lemieux, had diagnosed him with free floating anxiety. Raymond explained this was a diffuse, chronic sense of uneasiness and apprehension not directed toward any specific situation or object. "To put it another way, you might simply feel worried, nervous, and fearful for no apparent reason. It might be an imbalance of neurotransmitters. However, the most effective approach to handling this situation is to identify strategies to overcome it. While some individuals discover that exercise can alleviate the symptoms, others find solace in music or reading."

Carl knew the anxiety stemmed from the problems he was having with his wife, Andrea. The irony of having his colleagues holding him in such high esteem, while his wife had such a low opinion of him, made his anxiety worse. Surrounded by such positivity at the meeting, when his home life was miserable, made him feel like an imposter. Carl wandered into a large empty room and sat at a table by himself. He put his head in his hands and could feel the tears running down his face. He sobbed uncontrollably. After five minutes, he was able to pull himself together, and he stopped crying. Careful not to rub his eyes, he dabbed the wet cheeks with a Kleenex. *I mustn't let anyone see me like this.*

Carl got up and went back to the meeting.

Chapter 2

Carl arrived at his home on the outskirts of Guelph, Ontario, a town about a ninety-minute drive west of Toronto. He pulled up into his driveway. After he pushed the button of the garage door opener hanging from the sun visor, he watched the door retract and he backed his Tesla into the garage. He removed the recharging cord hanging on a hook and plugged it in to recharge the car overnight. He glanced over at Andrea's Porsche Boxster. It was less than a year old and cost him over $100,000. The bank was happy to give him the loan payable over the next five years at a fixed rate of 6.9% yearly interest. *There goes my 9.5% surgical fee increase.* He shook his head as a pang of anxiety passed through body. An empty feeling swept through the pit of his stomach, and he could feel his pulse race. Carl closed his eyes and took three deep breaths. The empty feeling in the pit of his stomach settled and his pulse slowed down over the next 60 seconds. *It worked this time.*

He closed the garage door as he entered the kitchen. In the kitchen, Andrea sat at the table, her head buried in her phone. Despite knowing that she would have heard the garage door open and the Tesla pull into the garage, she continued to ignore him, completely engrossed with her phone screen. Carl glanced at her as she sat there. The short pencil skirt she had on accentuated her slender body and ample hips. With just the right amount of makeup, she enhanced her face to bring out her captivating dark brown eyes, while drawing attention to her full lips adorned with a vibrant red gloss. Every strand of her hair was perfectly in place, flawlessly styled to perfection.

"Where the fuck were you?" Andrea said, without looking up. "You knew I was going out tonight."

"I told you I had my inaugural Surgical Society meeting as president today," he said. "I invited you to the banquet, but you turned it down."

"There you go again, putting me down for not playing the perfect wife in your fucked-up world. You can fuck off, you narcissist. It's always about you and how important you are, isn't it? Well, what about me for a change?"

Carl stared at Andrea. Raymond Lemieux's words swirled in his head. *"Don't engage with her. It will just add fuel to her rage and make her angrier."* Raymond explained to Carl, during one of their many tense therapy sessions, that his wife's emotional volatility wasn't his fault, his voice calm and measured against the backdrop of Carl's nervous fidgeting. The bite of her words, the unjust accusation of narcissism, left a deep wound in his soul, a cold ache spreading through him.

Andrea stared back at Carl. "What, you've got nothing to say? This is just like you, isn't it, you wimp? Afraid of your own shadow. Your asshole psychiatrist said not to engage, didn't he? You are too weak to make up your own mind. Well, he can fuck off too!"

Carl's eyes met Andrea's, a silent communication passing between them. Her face flushed crimson, her eyes blazing with anger as she became increasingly agitated and worked up. Last summer was when her cousin, Beata, paid a visit from her home in Poland. Beata, a revolutionary leader of the Underground Ukrainian Movement, played a pivotal and crucial role in providing essential support to the Ukrainian army's efforts. With captivating detail, Beata recounted her experiences crossing the border into Ukraine, where she delivered weapons and supplies crucial to bolstering the valiant efforts of the Ukrainian army fighting for their homeland. Andrea underwent a remarkable transformation as she listened to Beata's stories, becoming a person with a distinctly different character and outlook on life.

During a conversation one evening while lying in bed, Andrea proposed to Carl, "Why don't we visit my cousin, Beata, in Poland, and stay a month or longer? I am excited about the idea of getting involved and secretly smuggling weapons to aid the less fortunate individuals in Ukraine. Just imagine the immeasurable value and significance our lives would gain by actively taking part in and contributing to resolving a real-life struggle, making a tangible difference in the lives of others. I could finally discover a sense of meaning and direction in my life, a purpose that had previously eluded me. A fulfilling path for you could involve volunteering at a field hospital, where you'd perform surgery, directly helping the injured soldiers who require your expertise."

After pausing to weigh his options and consider the potential dangers, Carl finally replied, "The level of risk is unacceptable; it's simply too dangerous. We are the parents of young children. What would we do with them while we were away? I am concerned about what would happen to them should we meet our end on the battlefield; what kind of future would they face without our protection and guidance? I have too many responsibilities at work to take that much time off, unfortunately. Even the most noble of causes would not persuade my partners to extend coverage for a full month. It just wouldn't work."

Andrea's rage today was similar to the fit of anger she had experienced that evening, a comparable outburst of fury. The loudness of her yell was so intense that it had woke Carl Junior and Simone, who then ran into the bedroom, filled with fear. With a burst of anger and frustration, Andrea stormed from the bedroom, her footsteps echoing as she fled into the spare bedroom and slammed the door behind her. Trembling and crying, Carl Junior and Simone had crawled in with Carl, shaken and distressed by the commotion and chaos surrounding them. After Carl gently settled them, they snuggled close to him, finding comfort and safety in his arms, and soon fell into a peaceful sleep.

Carl's mind flipped back to the present as Andrea sprung to her feet and stormed into the garage. He heard the garage door open and the Boxter's smooth engine fire up. With a screech of the tires, the Boxter left the garage, and the door closed shortly afterwards. He could hear the engine get quieter as the car reached the end of the street, then silence. A pang of guilt swept through his body when he realized he felt relieved now she had gone for the night. He had the house to himself with his kids. The risk of another verbal attack had gone.

He slowly ascended the stairs to Carl Junior's room, his hand hovering over the doorknob, then opened the door. For his seventh birthday last month, they gave him a Gameboy, its bright screen promising hours of fun with friends. Carl Junior was fast asleep, his Gameboy lying on the bed beside him, its faint blue light illuminating the room. They allowed him only an hour of play each day, with a strict "no playing in bed" rule before sleep; the quiet of his room was oppressive. Carl smiled, a wave of peace washing over him, as he carefully placed the Gameboy on the shelf, the faint hum of the charger a comforting background noise. He gently kissed his son's forehead, the soft skin cool against his lips, and then quietly closed the door behind him as he left.

When he opened Simone's door, she was talking to her

stuffed giraffe, Bubbles. "Hi honey," he said to her. "Why aren't you sleeping?" he leaned over and kissed her forehead.

"I heard you and mommy arguing," she said. "I didn't like what she said to you. We're not allowed to swear, so why can she?"

Trying to change the subject, he said, "Do you want me to stay with you and we can tell Bubbles a bedtime story together?"

"I think Bubbles has had enough stories for one night," said the 4-year-old. "I just finished telling him one."

"Ok, can I sit with you while you fall asleep?"

Simone thought about that for a few seconds. "Why is mommy always mad at us?" she asked.

"Mommy is going through a rough time right now. We have to be patient. You know how frustrated you get when you don't want to eat your vegetables, well us adults also get frustrated about some things as well."

"Why would she say she wished we were never born?"

Carl felt a deep pain in the pit of his stomach. He could feel a tear well up from the depths of his eyes. "Ah honey, she doesn't mean that. She was having a bad day. That's all. You and Carl Junior are the best things that have ever happened to us. She loves you." Carl reached down and swept Simone into his arms.

"I love you, daddy," she said.

Carl could no longer hold back the tears and sobbed uncontrollably. He managed to speak between sobs. "I love you too, honey."

"Daddy, why are you crying?"

"I am crying because I love you so much. Sometimes that happens when you love someone." Carl wiped away the tears and looked intently at Simone. "The other thing is, I think I saw a mouse run into your armpit."

"Oh no, daddy," squealed Simone. "You can't check!"

"I have to. It was a little brown mouse, and he doesn't belong there! I need to get him out." Carl reached into Simone's armpit and tickled her. Delightful laughter and screams of pleasure came out of her as she tried to wiggle away. After 30 seconds, he said, "You are right. There is no mouse."

Simone settled, but kept a smile on her face. "See, I told you there was no mouse."

"I think I saw him go to the other side!" Carl reached into her other armpit and tickled. Simone again squealed with delight and laughter until he stopped. "Huh, that's funny, no mouse there either."

"I told you so!"

"Ok honey. I think it is safe for you to go to sleep now. The mouse must have run away." He pulled the covers over her as she lay down. She grabbed Bubbles and held him close to her chest. Carl watched as she fell asleep in less than a minute. He gave her one last kiss on her forehead and then left her room.

Carl realized how tired he was. It had been a busy day with the meeting. Tomorrow, with the clinical part of the program finished, he would spend all day in administrative meetings. It would begin promptly at 8 a.m. Most of the Surgical Society executives stayed at the hotel, but Carl would have an hour drive to get there. Fortunately, it would be Sunday, so the traffic would be manageable at 6:30 when he planned to leave. After a quick shower, he crawled into bed. He fell asleep within five minutes.

****

The bed moved ever so slightly and he knew it was Andrea. He opened his eyes and glanced at his cellphone on the charging stand. It was 3 a.m. He rolled over and saw Andrea on her side of the bed, curled in the fetal position, facing away from him. "Are you OK?" he asked.

She responded to his query with a grunt. He reached across and touched her shoulder. She brushed his hand away. She smelled of stale cigarettes and beer. Another night at a bar. He had stopped asking himself why. Was it the need for her to feel in control of her own life instead of adapting to his? Was she trying to stave off boredom? Did she lack meaning and importance in her own life? These were a few of the many questions that came to mind. Andrea had few friends; she'd deliberately severed all contact, leaving her isolated and alone. She had told Carl, her voice cracking with unshed tears, that no one understood the depth of her pain. Smiling politely, her friends played the parts of happy wives and mothers, a performance that she told him was both practiced and slightly strained. Andrea convinced herself there had to be something more meaningful than her current situation, a life filled with purpose and excitement. Raymond had cautioned him not to let her downward spiral drag him down there too.

His greatest concern was for the safety of the children, who might get pulled into the same hole into which she had descended.

Chapter 3

The laparoscopic tower in the operating room cast a dull light on the rest of the room. The three laparoscopic screens showed the magnified image of an inflamed appendix, swollen and red, but not ruptured.

"You know," said Margo, the scrub nurse. "We can always tell the size of a surgeon's penis by what size gloves he wears to operate."

"I'm not sure I like the way this conversation is going," said Carl, who was performing the surgery.

"I've been a scrub nurse for 22 years and I have never been wrong," Margo continued. "This particular instance illustrates the point. Dr. Jacobs, our patient has exceptionally large hands and wears the largest gloves we have, size 8 ½, but they still fit him tightly. When we uncovered the sheet to prep him for the surgery, it came as no surprise to any of us nurses what we witnessed. We needed an additional chlorhexidine pad to thoroughly clean all the hard-to-reach areas."

"What ever became of politically correct decorum in the operating room?" quipped Carl.

"Ha ha," laughed Margo. "When Steve Jacobs is awake, you can ask him about his political decorum. He is the king of vulgar and offensive language. He is always the first one to tell the most inappropriate jokes. Now that he is the one undergoing surgery to have his appendix removed, he would anticipate the same from us."

Carl shook his head. Even in this era of heightened social expectations, the operating room continued to be a hub for inappropriate sexual comments. Most doctors and nurses appeared unfazed by the banter. It seemed to alleviate some of the tension in the high-pressure surgical environment, so Carl was hesitant to confront the team. He knew it would be a matter of time before someone complained and he would get dragged into the fray. His strategy, for the time being, was to steer clear of the comments that were buzzing around, pretending as if he didn't hear them. A happy and functional surgical team was far more important to him than adhering to social expectations.

Looking at the monitor in front of him, Carl carefully dissected the appendix, separating it from the colon. The inflammation caused it to stick to the wall of the colon, but freeing it was not difficult. With precision, he divided the mesentery, taking the blood vessels supplying the appendix, and meticulously cleared the base of the appendix for the ligature suture. When the appendix was free, he placed it into a clear plastic surgical bag and pulled it out of the abdomen through the umbilicus. Carl passed the specimen to Margo and closed the small incisions. Once he had finished, he left the operating room to talk with Steve's wife while the surgical team applied the dressings and transported him to the recovery room.

"The surgery went well, Diane," he said to Steve's wife as he sat beside her in the surgical waiting room. "You will be able to take him home in a few hours."

"Oh shit, Carl," she said. "Can't you keep him for a few days? He's going to drive me nuts with his whining about pain. You should see him when he gets a cold. He is a firm believer in the 'misery loves company' edict."

"Ha ha," replied Carl. "You know you can always call me if you are worried about anything. I have my cellphone with me all the time."

"Ok, then, but if he complains too much, I might just drop him off at your house for a few days so I can get some peace and quiet."

Carl laughed. "You can come by anytime you like. You are always welcome."

Diane hugged Carl and then whispered, "Thanks for taking care of him. I was glad it was you doing the surgery. You are the one I trust the most. Thank you." Her eyes grew moist, and the gentle curve of her smile revealed how thankful she was, in a way that words couldn't express. Carl had confidence that she would do a good job of looking after Steve.

Steve and Diane had two kids who were the same age as his own children, creating a lively and bustling household. They used to have play dates when his kids were younger, but Andrea decided last year that she wanted to distance herself from everyone associated with the hospital, even the children of the doctors. A wave of sadness washed over him as he thought about the kids playing together in their backyard last summer while he barbequed steak for the adults and hotdogs for the kids. The warm sunshine and cold beer while laughing at Steve's funny stories in the operating room brought back happy memories for him.

He had hoped it was a passing phase, but Andrea remained adamant about cutting all her ties to the hospital. *"I am sick of being the surgeon's wife," she screamed at him after the guests had left. "I deserve better. See if you enjoy it when people refer to you as the Andrea's husband. Like an afterthought or a second-class citizen."*

He left the surgical waiting room and went to the recovery room to talk with Steve. Except for the bed with Steve, the recovery room was completely empty. Steve was sitting up in the bed talking with Valerie, the recovery room nurse. He was totally awake. They were sharing a laugh when Carl sat on the edge of the bed. Valerie walked to the desk to finish her charting on the computer.

"The surgery went well," Carl said. "The appendix, although

acutely inflamed, did not perforate. You should be able to go home in a few hours."

"Thanks Carl," he replied. "I am assuming you did it with a laparoscope?"

"Yes, it was straightforward. Three tiny cuts, that's all."

"Three cuts, you say? What are these Band-Aids on either side of my scrotum? You didn't mix me up with another patient and do a vasectomy by mistake?"

Carl furrowed his brows with concern. "What are you talking about?"

Steve looked to the left and then to the right to make sure no one was looking and then lifted his hospital gown to expose his scrotum. Two small Band-Aids covered each side of his scrotum, positioned where a vasectomy incision would be made. Carl reached down and peeled off the Band-Aids. There was no incision underneath. Carl let out a chuckle. "It looks like Margo was getting you back for all the vulgar jokes you tell in the operating room."

Steve let out a laugh. "That bitch! She got me good. Make sure she knows I won't forget what she did. Tell her I'll find a way to retaliate for threatening my boys!" Once again, his laughter burst out uncontrollably. The intense vibrations caused the bed sheet to slide off the bed and land with a soft thud on the floor. With a blank expression, he stared down at his toes, lost in thought. Bright pink nail polish adorning the toenails appeared to be what caught his attention.

"What the fuck?" he cried out. Carl glanced up at the commotion created at the nursing station by Steve's loud outburst. Valerie, along with two other nurses, came running over, thinking something was wrong. When they saw the pink nails, a chorus of laughter erupted simultaneously. In a matter of moments, a large group of nurses gathered around Steve, forming a crowd. Laughing and pointing, they joined him to witness the spectacle of his painted toenails. Chuckling to himself, Carl quietly slipped out of the recovery room.

"Hi doc," said a voice sitting in a chair just outside the recovery room. Carl glanced at the woman. Her blond hair hung loosely to her shoulders and framed her pretty face. She was young, perhaps mid twenties. Her blue eyes penetrating into Carl's as though she was trying to read his mind.

"Sabrina, why aren't you standing around Steve's bed in the recovery room laughing at him with the others?" he asked. "You had nothing to do with the pink nail painting, did you?

"Of course not." Sabrina waved her hand, her vibrant pink painted fingernails caught Carl's attention.

Carl laughed. "I should have known!"

"Ok, it was me. But he deserved it! We don't get an opportunity like this very often, and I would not let it slip by without taking full advantage of this. Let me get you a coffee as my punishment for defacing your patient." She hopped off the chair and grabbed his elbow. "For my bad behavior, I'm treating you to Starbucks."

While they strolled together, with her hand on his elbow, Carl noticed how her designer scrub suit hugged her tightly contoured body. As they made their way towards the coffee shop, she kept up the conversation. When he noticed her flawless skin and heard her Ukrainian accent, it awakened some deep-seated emotions he believed he had long suppressed. The gentle scent of her perfume, Chloe, he recognized from the hint of Jasmine Sambac that drifted from her and delicately made its way to his nostrils. As he was deep in thought about her, he suddenly heard Sabrina say, "Carl? Were you listening to me?"

He shook his head as if to get rid of the distraction that prevented him from hearing what she was saying. "Sorry, my mind had drifted. What was that?"

Sabrina stopped suddenly. "You men. The only time you guys seem to be engaged in conversations is when they revolve around inappropriate remarks about women."

"Ha ha," said Carl. "You've been the cleaner in the operating room for a year now and you hear everything. You must have noticed that I rarely engage in these kinds of discussions. Eventually, we'll all get in trouble for violating the hospital's harassment policy."

"Don't be such a prude. Is that the right word? Besides, all work and no play make for a dull boy." Sabrina smiled and looked in his eyes. "I asked you what you wanted me to get you at Starbucks?"

"I'll have a short latte. Thanks."

Sabrina ordered two short lattes, the rich aroma of freshly brewed coffee filling the air, and they sat at a cozy table by the window. "Thanks for the coffee," said Carl. "It should be me buying you a coffee, not the other way round."

Sabrina reached across and squeezed his hand. "Everyone deserves to be treated kindly occasionally. It's my pleasure. I get the sense that you are feeling a heavy burden of pressure. I can tell that you are under a lot of stress." She paused as she looked into Carl's eyes. Carl felt a sudden tightness in his chest. That his unstable emotions could be read so easily came as a shock. He felt his heart skip a beat.

"Don't be so shocked," she continued. "Prior to my escape from the Ukraine, I had been attending medical school in Kiev until the Russians invaded. I was in the last year. Reading and understanding people's emotions is something I excel at. I had aspirations of specializing in psychiatry through a residency program, but unfortunately, Putin's actions have caused my dreams to crumble."

Carl's eyes widened in astonishment as he looked at her. Although he worked with her in the operating room at least once per week for the past twelve months, he had no knowledge of her past. Between each case, she was to clean the operating room as part of her job. Because of its limited size and resources, the small hospital had only 4 operating rooms, which fostered a close-knit community where everyone knew each other. "I had no idea," he said. "Do you have plans to complete your studies?"

"I applied to medical school here but there is such competition for spots, I didn't have a chance. My plan is to return to Kiev when the war is over." She shook her head sadly. "Until that time arrives, my strategy is to stay afloat by working in the operating room. The thing I truly enjoy is being in the presence of the patients. It's possible that you are unaware of this, but the cleaning staff often builds a rapport with the patients, who feel comfortable sharing things with us they may not share with you. I am pretty good at identifying the ones that are over the top with anxiety. Sometimes, just by letting them talk and listening to them, it helps them settle. Maybe you need someone to talk to?"

"I've had a lot on my mind lately," said Carl. "Just working through some issues, but I'll be OK." Sabrina looked at Carl skeptically. He shifted the conversation to a safer topic, effectively changing the subject. "I hope all your dreams come true. One thing about life I have learned is that if you really want something and pursue it with vigor, good things will happen. I'm sure you'll be a success. You are very perceptive."

"Your patients admire you. They express their love and gratitude for the exceptional care you give." Sabrina smiled and looked at her watch. "Yikes! My break was over two minutes ago. I need to get back to the OR." She reached across the table and squeezed his hand. As she was leaving, she whispered in his ear. "Everything will be alright, you'll see."

Chapter 4

In the hospital parking lot, Carl reclined in his Tesla, feeling the smooth leather seats beneath him. Before heading home, he craved a few moments of solitude to collect his thoughts. His mind drifted back to the moment when he first laid eyes on Andrea, and he could vividly recall the warmth of her smile. It was in Bali, a dozen years ago, when he first experienced the enchanting beauty of the island's temples and the taste of its spicy cuisine.

In Christchurch, New Zealand, Carl dedicated a year to an enriching internship that broadened his medical perspective and introduced him to the breathtaking landscapes of the country. The clock was ticking as he had just 6 weeks to return to Toronto and embark on his General Surgery training residency. With no set plans, he embarked on his journey to Indonesia and Thailand, starting with a flight to Singapore on Air New Zealand. After spending a few days in the hustle and bustle of the big city, he found himself craving for a quiet beach. Filled with a sense of adventure, he decided to board the next Garuda Airlines flight, curious to discover where he would touch down. The next flight on the list was bound for Bali.

The flight, buzzing with the excited chatter of twenty-somethings and their anticipation for the island, beckoned him to join. They informed him that the ideal destination was Kuta Beach, known for its stunning shoreline. He could secure a hotel room directly on the beachfront for just $10 a night, allowing him to wake up to the sound of crashing waves. After spending the first few nights getting some much-needed rest, he found himself at the Pande N Lily Bar, savouring their renowned mushroom pizza and witnessing the mesmerizing sunset.

He noticed a group of Americans around his age, lounging on comfortable chairs, sipping beer, and admiring the vibrant colours of the sunset. He joined them, settling down on the last vacant chair with a sigh of relief. While the sun's imminent disappearance captivated him, someone suddenly stood directly in front of him, obstructing his view. A beautiful woman with long curls stood surrounded by the breathtaking hues of the spectacular sunset. The silhouette revealed a woman with a curvaceous figure, dressed in form-fitting shorts and a halter top. As the sun disappeared behind the horizon, her radiant smile completed the vivid image etched in his mind forever. This memory of the first time he met Andrea would always bring a smile to his face.

Carl was speechless when she asked, "Can I sit on the edge of your seat?"

Ignoring his silence, she sat and leaned against his shoulder, savouring the taste of her beer as she tilted her head back. She smelled like lilacs and lilies. "I'm Andrea," she whispered in his ear.

Carl managed to get himself together enough to say, "Carl."

The hours slipped away unnoticed as they engaged in animated discussions about a myriad of topics throughout the night. As a native of Toronto, she found herself intrigued by Carl's small-town origins in Guelph, a mere hour's distance from the city. Their shared dreams of travelling the world created an instant connection between them. They strolled back to her hotel on Kuta Beach. As the night wore on, their footsteps mingling with the sounds of laughter and music from nearby beach bars. The address, 69 Heavenly Passion Path, was one he would remember for life. When they arrived and he was about to say goodnight, she grabbed his hand and led him to her room.

They spent the next month basking in the sun on the beach during the day and indulging in passionate sex during the nights together. Carl felt like he was floating through a hazy dream. Her beauty was undeniable, radiating from every pore and captivating everyone who laid eyes on her. Her kind heart was evident in the way she treated everyone she met. She made him feel like he was on top of the world, treating him with boundless kindness and affection. Every day she would shower him with compliments, praising his prowess in the bedroom and admiring his handsome features and intellect that surpassed his age.

Having just completed her undergraduate degree in

computer science, Andrea was eager to begin her master's program back in Toronto. Andrea's intelligence and sensitivity were unlike anything Carl had ever experienced; her insights were brilliant, and her understanding of others was profound. Memories overwhelmed Carl: the majestic image of a goddess, the serene presence of an angel, and the exhilarating feeling of being in love.

The sound of crashing waves filled the air. After reaching the beach one morning, Andrea suggested they try surfing. New Zealand's frigid Antarctic waters tested Carl's resolve, but he'd mastered surfing in their chilling embrace during his year-long internship. The full wetsuit, with its thick neoprene hood and gloves, restricted movement, making the rides feel stiff and uncomfortable. Andrea, a natural athlete with her lithe figure and quickness, had taken surfing lessons when she first arrived in Bali. She quickly learned the basics of surfing. He watched, astonished, as Andrea gracefully positioned herself on her board, eyes fixed on the oncoming waves, then turned with practiced ease to catch them. With three powerful strokes of her arms, she launched herself to her feet, the spray of the three-foot wave covering her face as she rode it to the shore. When Carl tried to follow, a powerful wave broke, sending him tumbling head over heels along the sandy bottom, his surfboard flying away. The wave crashed, carrying his board back to shore, the salty spray stinging his face as he struggled to retrieve it. Disheartened by his swim back to shore, Carl lacked the motivation to return to the waves at the break. The morning sun warmed him as he sat on the beach, the air carrying the scent of the ocean. He watched, captivated, as Andrea gracefully rode the waves, her newfound skill a joy to behold. Not a single flaw marred her breathtaking beauty, nor the intoxicating feeling she inspired in Carl.

With the weight of her surfboard under her arm, she carefully set it down on the soft, yielding sand next to Carl. With a fierce energy, she straddled him, her lips finding his in a long, passionate kiss, the salty tang of their emotions adding intensity to the moment. After a few minutes, she stood up. "Come with me," she said, her smile warm as she took his hand, leading him to their romantic tent cabana, the gentle sounds of the ocean adding to the erotic atmosphere.

In the cabana, with the soft whispers from the gentle sway of palm trees and the warm feel of the sand beneath their naked bodies, Carl and Andrea spent two hours wrapped up together. The surfing had left her breathless, the adrenaline still coursing through her veins, fueling a passion Carl had never witnessed. As he lay exhausted on the beach towel, the warm sand clinging to his skin, he tried to imagine a life full of unbridled passion and happiness. In his mind, she was the epitome of perfection, the woman of his dreams, flawless in every aspect and exceeding all expectations.

The Downfall

Carl came to understand that having an amazing life lies in discovering that special someone who inspires you to become the best version of yourself, someone who brings out your full potential and helps you to flourish. He found himself hoping against hope that it would somehow continue, unwilling to accept its conclusion.

One afternoon, she returned to the room after Carl had woken from an afternoon nap. She said she didn't feel well, her face pale with her hand pressed to her forehead. Throughout the afternoon, relentless vomiting, diarrhea, and intense cramping plagued her every moment. Concern filled Carl's mind as he couldn't help but worry about her. He found a pharmacy and returned with Imodium for the diarrhea, a Zofran injection for the vomiting, and Pepto-Bismol, hoping it would alleviate both issues. It wasn't until two days later that she finally started showing signs of improvement. A few days after that, Andrea had a flight booked back to Toronto.

A tearful goodbye at the airport followed the promises to see each other when Carl arrived to start his surgical residency. Carl had a few days alone to reflect on his time with Andrea. He missed her terribly. He missed hearing her tell him how great he was at pretty much everything, yet something didn't seem quite right. They had only known each other for a few hours before they dove into a deep emotional attachment to each other. Although the experience was the best one of his life, it felt too unreal to be true. It was only years later, after much reflection and discussing the magical time with his psychiatrist, Ray, Carl realized he was chasing something in Andrea that perhaps didn't exist. Ray, too agreed, something did not seem right.

They took the next step in their relationship and moved in together a few years later, back in Toronto. After Carl completed his residency and Andrea earned her master's in computer science, they finally tied the knot. Despite the relationship never reaching the same level of passion and intensity as in Bali, Carl couldn't shake the memory of how she made him feel during that time. He yearned to experience those moments once more, the ones that filled his senses with joy and happiness. He patiently waited, his heart filled with a longing to return to those past times and experience them again.

As he drove home in the darkness of December, the 10-minute journey seemed to stretch on, creating a wave of anxiety that intensified with each passing moment, bringing back the empty feeling in the pit of his stomach. Carl did not know what to expect when he got home. He hoped if Andrea was home, she would go out for the night as she usually did. That would spare him from having to endure her incessant complaining about how awful things are for her. She would tell him how he must have spent the day revelling in the glory of being showered with praise. She believed he did not know what the real world was like. Carl backed his car into the garage and followed his same routine to recharge his Tesla.

Walking into the house, he entered the kitchen. "Daddy!" screamed Simone. She hopped off the barstool at the kitchen counter and ran to Carl. She leapt into his arms. Carl threw her in the air and caught her before giving her a big hug.

"Come back and finish your dinner, Simone. You promised to eat one more carrot," said Andrea.

Simone pouted and looked at her dad. "Simone, you heard what your mother said. One more carrot and you are done," said Carl. Simone trudged back to her barstool and sat with her knees under her. She made a face and picked up the carrot. She put it in her mouth, chewed it and swallowed.

"Good girl," said Andrea. "You can leave the table now and get ready for bed. You too Carl Junior. Time to get ready for bed. Put your Gameboy down. Your hour of play is up."

"Ah mom, just another five minutes?" asked Carl Junior.

"You know the rules, Carl Junior," replied Andrea. "Give it to me." Carl Junior reluctantly passed it to his mother. In the kitchen, she found an outlet on the counter and plugged it in, the faint humming of the charger filling the room. "I removed the charger from his bedroom to reduce temptation," explained Andrea.

Carl Junior went upstairs to his bedroom. "We'll be up to say good night in a few minutes," said Andrea.

With a sigh, Andrea gathered the children's dishes from the cluttered kitchen counter and placed them in the dishwasher. With a cloth in hand, she diligently wiped the counter, gathering all the crumbs. Once finished, she rinsed the cloth and neatly draped it over the facet. Carl watched in silence as she cleaned, uncertain what might come next. Andrea stopped what she was doing and glanced at Carl and stared at him for a moment before she said, "We need to talk."

Carl felt the familiar empty pit in his stomach as a wave of anxiety washed over him. "Let's sit over here," he said as he pointed to the chairs around the kitchen table. Positioned across from him, Andrea joined him at the table, creating a physical separation between them. She looked at him and took an enormous sigh.

"This life we have together is not working out for me," she said. Andrea paused and took a big breath, as if gathering her thoughts before continuing. She cast a quick downward glance at her hands, like she was searching for a script to read from. Carl remained silent to see which direction this conversation was going. In the past, he had suggested marital counselling, but she said he was the one with the problem. Following that conversation is when he met with his colleague, Dr. Raymond Lemieux, a psychiatrist. Ray had proved very helpful in helping him navigate the marital strife while continuing to function in his highly stressful job as a surgeon.

"What are you thinking we should do?" asked Carl. Being a surgeon, his daily routine revolved around problem-solving. This was something in which he had always excelled, finding solutions to complex problems. His anxiety faded away as he saw this as a step forward for his marriage. *Working in unison, they could overcome this obstacle. Andrea wanted to talk it out. There was hope.*

"I want a divorce."

Carl felt the empty feeling in the pit of his stomach return. His heart raced as anxiety took over. He felt his eyes flicker back and forth. He had difficulty catching his breath and a tightness developed in his chest. *This can't be happening.*

"Let's talk this through, Andrea," he said, his voice filled with concern. "We can work this out if we put in the effort and communicate openly with each other. Can you please tell me what you want me to do? I am willing to do whatever it takes. You can get a job in software development, like you always wanted. You are always getting recruiters asking you to join them and you can do that now. The kids are older. Have you considered the children's needs and well-being in this situation? We have a great life here. We can work together to find a solution." Carl was babbling in a desperate effort to evade comprehending what she had uttered. "Let's seek someone we can engage for a meaningful dialogue and find a solution."

Andrea's brow furrowed as she shook her head. "It's too late. The time for talk is gone. I cannot live like this any longer. We revolve our life around you as a surgeon. You spend all day at the hospital. Every fourth night, you are on call. It's like a chain around my ankle. The entire world thinks you are wonderful, while I see my life as an individual slip away. I crave for recognition and appreciation that I will never see while married to you. You will always be the one to steal the spotlight. I can't be my best person while you get all the glory."

With every word she spoke, Carl felt his entire life crumbling away, like a fragile house of cards. He had always hoped that she would see as shared successes his successes. It was beyond his understanding why she would feel the way she did. Despite having two beautiful children, financial security, and respect in the community, she still felt that something was missing. Many people considered this life to be a dream come true, but deep-down Carl knew her true dreams were elsewhere. It was entirely her choice to dedicate herself to being a stay-at-home mom and focus on her family. Given her impressive skills as a software developer, job opportunities sought after her, barraging her email inbox. She could have easily secured a position at any of the many companies actively seeking individuals with her expertise. Carl's mind was completely void of any thoughts or ideas, leaving him unable to articulate a single word.

"I met someone," said Andrea as she glanced down at her hands. "He wants us to start a company together. He's done it before, a software company. I'll be the CEO and managing director. I'll be moving with the kids to Toronto. You'll be less than an hour away, so you'll see Carl Junior and Simone often enough."

Carl thought for a moment, shaking his head. "It's too sudden. Who is this guy, anyway? How do you know you can trust him? There is no way he could take care of the kids and love them as much as I do. Andrea don't do this. Please."

"You can look him up on the internet. Jacob Freisner, a successful software developer. Jacob Freisner's companies have a valuation of $100 million. I'm moving this weekend. You can keep the house for now, but we'll sell it in a few years when the kids are a little older. That way, when they stay with you on weekends, they will feel at home."

Defeat washed over Carl, leaving him feeling discouraged and disheartened. It dawned on him that attempting to change her mind would be futile. It was obvious now to Carl she had been planning this for some time. While he had his head buried in the sand, with the hope she would turn around to see things his way, she had all along been scheming to exit. Along with the humiliation of her cheating, he felt like a fool for thinking she was just going through a phase.

As these emotions ran through him, he couldn't help but put his head in his hands. The constriction in his chest made it difficult for him to take a deep breath. The intense feeling of self-loathing washed over him as he reflected on his weakness in the presence of Andrea. He wasn't sure how much more he could take. Andrea stood up from the table, making her way towards the stairs, intending to say goodnight to the kids. At the foot of the staircase, she turned and said, her voice filled with determination, "I have a lawyer and she has crafted a separation agreement. I suggest you get advice from a lawyer as well."

As she made her way up the stairs, Carl burst into tears.

Chapter 5

The band's loudness drowned out any possibility of engaging in conversation. It suited Carl just fine, as he wasn't in the mood to engage in any discussion. Three weeks had passed since Andrea left the house. To minimize disruption for the children, she agreed to leave them with Carl until after the Christmas break. Carl had arranged for a babysitter so he could attend the hospital's annual Christmas party.

Someone yelled something in his ear, but he could not make it out because of the loud music. Carl pointed to his ear and then to the band and shrugged his shoulders. It was Steve Jacobs. The music stopped as the band announced they would be right back after a quick break. Steve said, "I feel great since my appendectomy. What did you do to me in there? My bowels move every morning, and my chronic constipation is gone."

Carl laughed and said, "I didn't come here to the party to talk about your personal toiletry habits, but it's good to hear you are doing well."

"Where's Andrea?"

Except for his psychiatrist, Carl had yet to tell anyone about Andrea moving out. "She couldn't make it," he replied. They talked for a few minutes before Steve headed back to his table. Carl glanced at his watch. It showed 8:01. He needed to get back home to be sure his kids were in bed and asleep so they would be ready for school tomorrow. Carl said goodbye to those around him and headed off towards the exit.

The party took place in a spacious banquet hall that was on the outskirts of town. After giving the attendant his ticket, he retrieved his coat and was about to leave when he heard a familiar voice. "Hey doc," said the voice.

Carl turned around. It was Sabrina. She wore a form-fitting red skirt and a tight white blouse that accentuated her curves. Her blonde hair cascaded down her shoulders, framing her face. With bright red lipstick that perfectly complemented her short skirt, she looked stunning. Her familiar scent of Jasmine Sambac, her Chloe perfume, filled the air, gently reached his nose. "You look like you are ready to leave," she said. "Would you mind giving me a lift into town? It would save me from calling an Uber."

Carl took a step backwards and glanced at Sabrina. "You certainly got dressed up for the occasion. Why would you want to leave so early?"

"I was sitting with the cleaning staff team, who had indulged in a bit too much alcohol. Their boisterous behavior became more apparent as the night went on. The inappropriate comments crossed the line. I felt uncomfortable. I decided to leave before I smacked one of them."

"Ha ha," laughed Carl. "I am happy to give you a lift."

Carl anxiously shifted his weight from one foot to the other, his gaze unwavering as Sabrina momentarily disappeared to retrieve her coat. They headed to his car.

"Wow!" she exclaimed, "A Tesla. I have always wanted to get a ride in one of these."

Carl opened the passenger door, and she hopped in. He walked over to the driver's seat and sat down and started the car.

"Why are you leaving so early?" asked Sabrina as they drove away.

"I left my kids with a babysitter and I want to make sure they get to bed on time," he replied.

"Your wife not around?"

Carl sighed. Stricken with shame, he placed the blame squarely on his own shoulders for the failure of his marriage. He was uncertain if he could discuss it with Sabrina without revealing his vulnerabilities. Although he felt safe talking about his failed marriage with Ray, he wasn't sure he could discuss it with anyone else. He struggled to find some words that could convey reassurances he was alright, but none came to mind.

"I sense your stress levels are off the chart," continued

Sabrina. "It really helps to talk about it. Your wife left you, didn't she?"

Carl glanced at Sabrina incredulously. *Am I that transparent? How could she possibly know? I have told no one at the hospital. I had planned to keep it to myself until I felt more comfortable with what had happened. Was Sabrina just guessing? There is no way Andrea would have discussed this with anyone at the hospital.* "How did you know?" he asked.

"I have observed you over the past 6 months and I have seen your stress levels rise. Most people, especially men, are not aware of the non-verbal clues that give it away. For example, I have seen you during an operation when your eyes would flicker away from the laparoscopic screen as if distracted. Sometimes, you take a deep sigh for no reason, a sure sign of anxiety. Other times, when you are standing around, you struggle to find a comfortable place to put your hands."

"How does all that lead you to the conclusion that Andrea left me?"

"Many other reasons for stress dissipate over time. The death of a loved one, financial burdens, health worries, are examples. When a good man suffers marital problems, the stress may linger for years."

Carl had arrived in the center of town. "Turn right on Main

Street," instructed Sabrina. "110 is halfway down. I am staying in a basement apartment of a brick house." Carl turned onto Main Street. "Could you drive around to the back?"

Carl pulled into the driveway and stopped at the back of the building. "So, do you want to talk about it with me? I am not getting out until you say something."

Sabrina gazed directly into his eyes. They were soft and betrayed compassion. Before he knew what had happened, he began his story. Once Carl started talking, his words poured out like a rushing river, unstoppable. Driven by an intense desire, he yearned to unburden himself and share his suffering with someone. Sabrina quietly listened. When he got to the part where Andrea was starting her own company and moving in with another man, Carl stopped, unable to continue.

"I think she has done you a favour," said Sabrina. "This could have continued for a few more years of suffering for you, but she has severed the relationship definitively. She is giving you permission to move on."

"I suppose you're correct in that aspect. Right now, I'm unsure if I'm ready to move on. It seems like I need some extra time to figure things out."

"I've seen the way you look at me. You need to be honest with yourself. I think you are ready now." She reached over and grabbed his hand. "Kiss me." Sabrina leaned over to the diver's side and planted her soft lips against his. Carl responded by opening his mouth and she slid in her tongue. Carl could feel himself getting aroused. It had been over 12 months since he had sex and it was almost as if he could not control his passion. Sabrina was right. He hadn't been this excited around a woman for years. The kissing was becoming more intense as she reached around his head and forced his lips firmly on hers.

Carl reached up with his right hand and slid it under her blouse. She was not wearing a bra. He could feel her aroused nipple under his fingers as he cupped her left breast in his hand. The breast was the perfect size and could fit in a champagne glass. The warmth from his hand seemed to flow through to the rest of his body.

Suddenly, Sabrina released the hold she had on Carl's head and pulled away from him. Carl removed his hand from her breast. Sabrina said, "I must go now." With no further explanation, she exited from the passenger side of the car. Carl watched as she opened the door with her key and walked into her apartment.

He started the car and drove home.

Chapter 6

Carl was finishing a laparoscopic sigmoid colon resection when his cellphone rang. Margo, who was the circulating nurse that day, answered it for him.

"Dr. Carl Mackenzie's phone," she said. Margo listened for a while and then continued, "He's just finishing his last case. Yeah, I'll let him know to drop by your office."

"Who was that?" asked Carl.

"Barry Little wants you to drop by his chief of staff office after you finish," replied Margo.

He probably wants me to see one of his hypochondriacal relatives again. The last one was certain she had colon cancer, even after I did a normal colonoscopy.

Everything went smoothly during the laparoscopic colon resection surgery, and the outcome was a success. The results of a pre-operative CAT scan showed that there was no metastatic disease in the liver. During the dissection, one of the crucial steps was locating the inferior mesenteric vessel as it exited the aorta and then carefully applying clips to secure the artery before proceeding to divide the vessel. Carl demonstrated great attention to detail by carefully identifying the left ureter to avoid any potential injury. After carefully tying off the blood supply to the tumour, he divided the mesentery and stapled the colon, ensuring a 10 cm margin on both sides of the tumour.

Using a small incision above the bladder, Carl skillfully removed the segment of sigmoid colon that contained the cancer, as well as the regional lymph nodes. After the successful removal, he proceeded to staple the bowel back together, taking great care in the process.

The cancer journey had brought him close to the patient and his family. Knowing that they had faith in him, Carl felt a deep sense of responsibility to guide them safely through this. With eager anticipation, he was excited to share the good news with Ruby, the beloved wife, who anxiously awaited the news in the surgical waiting room.

After writing the post-operative orders, Carl walked to the surgical waiting room. "The surgery went well. There was no spread that I could see," Carl said to Ruby, who had been pacing around the room and hallway.

Carl beckoned her to sit down in the chairs. He continued, "The pathologist will examine the lymph nodes to be certain there is no microscopic spread of cancer. There is a very good chance the surgery cured him."

Carl saw a tear form in the corners of her eyes and roll down her cheeks. He reached for the small pack of tissues he carried specifically for this purpose and gave her one. She grabbed his hand and said, "Thank you, thank you. You have saved his life."

"I'll talk with you again once I have more information," said Carl. "You can see him in a few minutes in the recovery room. I expect you will be able to take him home tomorrow." She gave a hug to Carl and thanked him again.

Still dressed in his surgical scrub suit, Carl walked down the hallway to Barry Little's office. Barry, a diminutive endocrinologist with round horn-rimmed glasses in his early sixties, stood up and shook his hand, pointing to the chair beside him.

"Thanks for speaking with me on such short notice," said Barry. Barry glanced at the papers on his desk with a concerned look on his face.

Barry's formality caught Carl off guard. Barry was someone he had known his entire life. Carl's father and Barry shared a close friendship. They were inseparable golfing buddies, and they dedicated every Sunday afternoon to their time on the golf course. It was Barry who provided the encouragement and motivated Carl to embark on a career in medicine. Once Carl completed his residency in surgery, Barry took the initiative to recommend hiring Carl to join the hospital staff.

"What's this about, Barry? Is there a problem?" asked Carl.

Barry sighed and said, "There has been a complaint. Our HR department has thoroughly reviewed it, and the lawyer has consulted with the union. The union has agreed to let us handle the complaint, but if they don't agree with the direction it's going, they will step in, which is something we desperately want to avoid."

Carl's body tensed up and his pulse skipped a beat. He could feel the hollow sensation in the pit of his stomach intensify. He stared at Barry, his heart pounding in his chest, dreading what was about to escape from his lips. Barry seemed uncertain how to start as his eyes darted around the room. His right leg bounced up and down, something Carl knew he did when he was uncomfortable.

"I'll get right to the complaint." Barry cleared his throat before he began. "One of our cleaning staff, Sabrina Hawryluk, claims you touched her breast after you drove her home the night of the Christmas party last week."

Carl breathed a sigh of relief. "That's the complaint? That is ridiculous. I have told no one here yet about what has been going on in my life, so you'll be the first one. Andrea left me for a multi-millionaire software engineer about a month ago. She moved to Toronto. I went to the Christmas party alone and left at 8 p.m. As I was leaving, Sabrina asked if I could drop her off at her apartment on the way home. When I told her I was leaving early to put my kids to bed, she arrived at the conclusion my wife had left me and asked me to tell her the story about what happened. When I finished telling her, she asked me to kiss her, so I did. The kiss went on for longer than I had anticipated and was quite passionate. I thought she was going to ask me into her apartment and yes, I touched her breast. She said she had to go after that. We said good night. I haven't seen her since. End of story."

Carl was breathless as he finished. Barry stared at Carl without emotion. *What the hell was the matter with Barry?* "Look," Carl continued, his eyes pleading for understanding. "If it helps, I'm happy to swallow my pride and apologize to her. I thought that was what she wanted. I didn't mean to offend her. This is simply a case of miscommunication, no need to overcomplicate it."

"How about we ask the HR lawyer to come up so you can explain it to her and we can work out a resolution? It sounds innocent enough to me." Barry picked up the phone and punched in the extension. "Steph, can you come up to my office? I have Carl with me." Barry replaced the phone to cradle and said to Carl, "She'll be right up."

Carl and Barry sat in silence, each lost in their own thoughts, the weight of the moment hanging heavily in the air. Stephanie Laurenson entered through the open door approximately three minutes later. After exchanging handshakes with Carl during the introductions, she took a seat across from him.

"Barry filled you in about the complaint?" asked Stephanie.

Carl nodded, saying nothing. Despite feeling embarrassed about his circumstances, he aimed to mitigate any harm to his reputation. If it meant having a rational discussion at this level, he would not hesitate to recount his story in order to expedite the resolution of this matter.

"Are you comfortable telling me what happened?" asked Stephanie.

"Absolutely," replied Carl. "I have done nothing wrong." Carl recounted his story about what happened but added a few more details such as Sabrina's ability to read non-verbal clues to arrive at her conclusion he was under stress and that she wanted to help.

Stephanie made some notes as he spoke. When he finished, Carl said, "I'm happy to apologize to her. I did not mean to offend her. What do I need to do for a rapid resolution to this?"

Stephanie glanced up at Carl. "Not that simple." She shook her head. "What you did in the car that night constituted sexual assault. You touched her breast without her permission. We had no choice but to ask her to file a police report accusing you of sexual assault. You will need to get a lawyer and..." A sudden outburst from Carl interrupted her words.

"Are you out of your fucking mind?" he shouted. "She is the

one who asked me to kiss her. We are both adults. I stopped when she said she had to go. What the fuck did she expect?"

Stephanie's face flushed a deep shade of crimson. A shadow passed over her face, causing her eyes to darken. Her finger pointed directly at Carl as she shouted, "You are not still in high school. Engaging in sexual assault against women is unacceptable and unlawful. What kind of foolish person are you to engage in such behavior and believe it is acceptable? What planet do you live on? Wake up and open your eyes, you idiot. You are in a heap of trouble!"

Carl could feel panic rise in his chest, making it hard to breathe. Stephanie stood up and stormed out of the room. Carl glanced at Barry, who seemed consumed by something in his papers, refusing to meet his stare. "Barry," said Carl. "She cannot be serious. This is crazy." Carl held his head in his hands. He felt the tingling anxiety consume his body as he sat there in silence.

Barry finally spoke. "Call the Canadian Medical Protective Association and ask them for advice."

Carl got up from the chair, saying nothing else. *This has been the worst day of my life. I've done nothing wrong. What is going on? Why is all this happening to me?*

Chapter 7

"We have to be prepared for the next step the hospital intends to take," said Michael Smithers, the lawyer assigned to help Carl from the Medical Protective Association. "Undoubtable they will attempt a mid-term suspension of your privileges, now that you have declined to take a voluntary leave of absence."

As they sat on the 47th floor of the TD Tower in downtown Toronto, Carl listened to the words, but his mind was elsewhere. He marveled at the breathtaking view of the cityscape below through the floor to ceiling windows. The magnificent view of Lake Ontario and the Toronto Island stretched out before him. While he processed Michael's words, his gaze shifted towards the shimmering water.

During the past summer, he had sailed his 35-foot sailboat to Toronto Island and spent a week there with Andrea and their two children. He could see the spot they had moored for the week along the break wall of the inner channel at Hanlon's point. Andrea had taken a break in her constant fighting with him for that week, and he felt a glimmer of hope they could salvage their marriage. The warm sun shone every day. The memory of the perfect weather and of the laughter of his children running on the sandy beaches brought a smile to his face. Despite the sunny weather today, the chilly December air kept the docks deserted.

"Are you sure you wouldn't rather take a voluntary leave of

absence?" asked Michael. "The hospital will be obliged to report their decision of mid-term suspension to the College of Physicians and Surgeons, and they could decide to remove your license to practice."

Carl sighed deeply. He turned his gaze from the window and faced Michael. "By taking a leave of absence, won't it seem like I am admitting to doing something wrong?"

Michael thought about that for a moment. "Rest assured, as your lawyer, my primary objective is to protect you and ensure that the process causes you as little harm as possible. The direction that this is going in is quite uncertain and it is challenging to determine what will happen. Regardless of whether the police report is dismissed, the hospital still has a duty to address and resolve the issue. What you need to understand is within every system, there is a structured hierarchy of power. In terms of social hierarchy, society often regards doctors as occupying the highest position, while unionized floor cleaners could be perceived as occupying the lowest position. Those in positions of power within an organization may often exploit employees, particularly those who are vulnerable or lack authority themselves. Anticipating accusations like this is crucial for us."

"So now I'm a sexual predator preying upon the weak." Carl shook his head. "This is so wrong. That is not what happened."

"There is something else," said Michael. He cast his gaze downwards towards the pile of papers on his desk, seemingly searching for the right words to express himself. "The Medical Protective Association will only defend the medical and hospital related legal issues. You are going to need legal counsel if the police file sexual assault charges. I have asked my criminal lawyer partner to meet with you after we have finished. He will give you advice on what you should do if that happens."

"This gets worse and worse," said Carl. His chest became tight and he was having difficulty breathing. "You mean I could go to jail?"

"Look," said Michael. "I'll let you discuss it with my partner. For my part, I would ask you to think about taking a voluntary leave of absence to avoid the unnecessary publicity that would accompany a mid-term suspension. I think that would be the best plan with the least chance of harm. Maybe we could talk about it over the phone tomorrow?"

Carl's mind was spinning. He needed to get outside in the cold air and take a deep breath. *The situation could be easily fixable through a simple conversation, yet all the lawyers said it had gone past that stage. Perhaps I could have a private conversation with Sabrina and persuade her to reveal that she was the one who instigated what happened, not me. But everyone has repeatedly cautioned me against reaching out to her, as it would only escalate the situation. They let me know she was unavailable and on stress leave from work.* His mind was a chaotic storm of thoughts, desperately trying to find a solution that stubbornly evaded him.

Michael was on the phone asking his partner to come into the conference room. A minute later, a tall man with salt and pepper hair wearing an expensive business suit walked into the room. He walked up to Carl as he stood up from the chair and reached for his hand. "I'm Martin Wheeler," he said as they shook. His grip was firm and confident. "I am going to spend an hour with you," he said, "and during that time, we can discuss a few things. I understand that you've recounted the story multiple times, but could you please provide me with a detailed account of what occurred?" Michael bid them farewell and exited the room, leaving them to have a private conversation.

Carl repeated the story. Martin took a few notes, but listened intently. When Carl finished, Martin put down his pen and said, "That is quite the story. Any idea why she would make a complaint?"

"I've been racking my brain," answered Carl. "There are a few thoughts that come to mind. Perhaps she wants money. But if that were the case, I would have expected her to approach me directly, and she didn't. Perhaps she confided to a friend at the hospital and the HR department put pressure on her to report it to set an example. Really, I do not know why she would do this." Carl shook his head and glanced at his hands. "Is there something I can do to make this all go away? Can I offer to pay her?"

"The answer to both questions is no. Almost certainly, the police will lay charges of sexual assault," replied Martin. "I have handled many cases similar to this. The courts have a responsibility to address and take seriously any complaints of non-consensual sexual touching. It will be up to a judge to decide if this meets the threshold of sexual abuse. If the police arrest you, they will take you to the precinct for fingerprinting and processing. It is important that you say nothing without me present. Here is my card with my office, cell phone and home number. They will allow you to call me."

Carl felt his heart skip a beat. His chest constriction returned, and he again felt he couldn't breathe. "Maybe I should leave the country? It sounds so unfair. I did nothing wrong."

"This is the legal system. In recent times, there has been a significant focus on highlighting and holding individuals accountable for engaging in inappropriate sexual behavior. Regrettably, in the absence of explicit verbal consent, the law remains unequivocal. Engaging in sexual touching without consent is strictly prohibited. Even if done passionately, kissing is not categorized as sexual touching."

"Oh, my God. What has become of spontaneity? How much worse could this get?"

Martin looked at Carl with sadness in his eyes. "You could go to jail for one to five years. They would have you registered in the national sexual offender's registry, which is shared with every country in the world. Other countries could prohibit you from travelling. That is why we must defend this vigorously."

Carl shook his head. "You are going to help me? How much will it cost?"

Martin sighed. "You will need to send me a retainer for $100,000. I expect the total cost will be close to $500,000."

The shock that ran through Carl's body was so intense that it made his heart skip a beat. Upon realization, he quickly understood that this was a matter far more serious than he had initially expected. He was on the brink of having his entire life utterly destroyed. He was determined not to let all his hard work from his entire life slip away just because of a momentary lapse in judgment that lasted only ten seconds. *Martin was right. I have to defend myself. My line of credit needs to be increased. I need to do it fast. The house serves as collateral for the line of credit. Andrea will want her share of the house.*

"I don't have that kind of money. I need to speak with my bank manager," said Carl.

"My advice is to do it as soon as possible, so we are ready when the police come to arrest you."

With a heavy heart, Carl bid Martin bid farewell, their words lingering as he left the lawyer's office. The drive home was a frustrating two-hour journey, with the constant honking and exhaust fumes filling the air. Carl parked his Tesla in the garage. In approximately thirty minutes, the bus would arrive to drop off the children. Suddenly, the doorbell broke the silence, echoing through the house. Carl went to answer, feeling the weight of anticipation in his chest.

"You are under arrest for sexual assault," the police officer stated firmly, his words hanging heavy in the air. Placing handcuffs on his wrists, he led him to the police cruiser.

Chapter 8

Carl realized it was not possible to prepare oneself for the humiliation and degradation of an arrest. The local newspaper had reporters waiting for him when he arrived at the precinct. As soon as the police car door opened and he stepped onto the sidewalk, cameras flashed, and a barrage of questions flew at him. "Tell us what happened," yelled the reporter. "Are you guilty of what they say? Sexual assault."

Carl tried to hide his face with his handcuffed wrists, but he knew it was useless. The news outlet in his community would plaster his picture, making headline news. As far back as anyone could remember, no prominent high-profile person had experienced an event even remotely similar. They led him into the precinct. After the fingerprinting and the picture taking, they allowed him to make a phone call to Martin.

"They were waiting for me when I got home," he said. "I tried to get them to wait for my children to get home on the bus from school, but they left a female police officer instead. They allowed me to call Andrea. She didn't pick up, so I left a message with the police officer's cell phone number. They took my phone away after that, so I couldn't call you until now."

"Remember what I said," replied Martin. "Say nothing. I'm on my way to the precinct now. I expect they will take you to a jail cell. We can talk after I arrive."

As the police escorted Carl to the jail cell, the heavy metal door creaked open. It wasn't until he entered the room that they finally offered to take off the handcuffs, easing his discomfort. Placing both wrists through the opening in the bars of the door, he felt a sense of relief as the officer removed the cuffs. The powerful scent of bleach permeated the dimly lit cell. They had meticulously scrubbed and polished the room until it sparkled. A subtle odor of vomit and urine mingled with the bleach. As the feeling of nausea washed over him, Carl could taste bile creeping up his throat, intensifying the urge to vomit. To suppress the urge to vomit, he took deep breaths, trying to regain control. After a few minutes, the churning in his stomach settled, and he felt a sense of relief.

Hanging from one wall was a metal framed bed, its mattress covered in a crisp, clean cotton sheet. Carl sat on the bed. Now that he was alone, his racing pulse had calmed, but the lingering tightness in his chest refused to dissipate. He could be stuck here, waiting for hours or even days, before they finally release him. With nothing to do, he lay on the bed and stared at the ceiling. He closed his eyes, seeking solace from the overwhelming waves of anxiety. The scene where the police officer arrested him replayed in his mind, each detail vivid and haunting. It felt like a perpetual loop, playing out repeatedly with no variation. Whenever he revisited the scene where the police officer cuffed his wrists, a wave of anxiety coursed through his body, causing a sharp pain in his abdomen.

"Your lawyer is here to see you," said a voice on the other side of the cell. Carl sat up. *I must have fallen asleep.*

As Carl placed his hands through the hole in the bars, he felt the cold metal of the cuffs closing tightly around his wrists. The officer guided him through a labyrinth of corridors and doors until they reached a cramped interrogation room. In front of a table, Martin sat on a chair, his gaze fixed on the papers scattered across its surface. As soon as Carl entered the room, he stood up from his seat with concern on his face. As the officer removed the cuffs, Carl took a seat across from Martin, feeling a mix of relief and apprehension.

"Are you okay?" asked Martin.

"A little shaken up, but I am managing," Carl replied.

"They told me you were concerned about your kids. Andrea is with them at the house. She came right away from Toronto. They are fine."

"I do not think Andrea will take this well." Carl could only imagine the shock she must be experiencing upon learning about his arrest for sexual assault. This would strengthen her determination to create more distance between them. Shame washed over him as he thought about the effect this would have on Andrea. Even worse, she would prohibit him from seeing their children. Being on the registered sexual offender list would give her the necessary grounds to pursue full custody.

"My aim is to get you out on bail," said Martin. "There will be a bail hearing tomorrow. With a reasonable judge, we can have you out by noon tomorrow. You'll have to spend the night here, though."

Carl sighed, his shoulders slumping as he exhaled. He had expected that, and a sigh of relief escaped his lips. Staying here would be a wise decision, as it would provide him with a shield against the intrusive press. If his colleagues asked about what happened, he had no idea what he would say. While in prison, he took comfort knowing that he was out of reach of everyone. He could use the time to reflect on what he wanted to say. It would be ideal if everyone could ignore him and he wouldn't have to say anything.

"Let me tell you what you can expect tomorrow. The police will drive you to the courthouse and escort you inside. There is a prep room where you will meet me. I looked at the court docket, and so far you are the only one, so I expect we'll be first. The judge will read the charges to you. As this is a bail hearing, the judge will hear arguments from the crown and then myself. Given your reputation in the community and low flight risk, the judge will likely ask for a

$100,000 bail. Do you have questions?"

Carl shook his head. "Thanks for coming. I'll look forward to seeing you tomorrow."

Once they bid each other farewell, the officer returned Carl to the cell. As he lay on the mattress, he noticed the cracks and imperfections in the ceiling above him. To his surprise, his anxiety had lessened. With no one around, he relished the tranquility of solitude. He closed his eyes and in less than 30 seconds he was asleep.

After what seemed a few minutes, a loud noise woke him up. "Get your fucking hands off of me," yelled the voice. "This is police brutality!"

Carl heard a loud clang as the cell door next to him swung open. The man said, "I don't think I want to go in there." He was slurring his words.

"Look," said the police officer to the man, "if you go in there, I'll remove your cuffs and you can go to sleep in the comfortable bed."

A few moments of silence followed before the man replied, "OK, then. I'll go."

Carl heard the door close and the sound of a key in the cuffs. The cuffs jangled as the officer replaced them on his belt. The man started singing. It sounded like an Irish ditty. Something about an Irish Rover.

"Shut the fuck up!" yelled another voice from down the hall. This seemed to encourage him to sing even louder. Shortly after, additional individuals started yelling at him to cease singing, yet he persisted. The noise was incredibly loud, making it impossible to sleep. Carl stared at the ceiling, looking at the complex patterns. He could feel his chest tightening and had difficulty catching his breath. His pulse raced. He questioned his ability to withstand any further strain, unsure of how much more he could bear. Even with his eyes closed, he couldn't escape the relentless barrage of noise. The weight of anxiety and humiliation only heightened his stress.

He needed to fight this baseless accusation with all his might and get his life back.

Chapter 9

Breakfast came at 7:30 a.m. The clanging sound echoed through the prison as the guards pushed the tray through the slot in the bars of the front door. Carl had eaten nothing since he ate the sandwich given to him at the lawyer's office the day before. It felt like such a long time had passed, although it had been less than 24 hours. Despite lacking any appetite, he reasoned he needed to eat something to maintain his strength. Carl took the cold metal tray and sat on the bed. He removed the tray cover. In the center of the metal plate sat a limp, yellow pancake, its edges slightly curled from moisture. Flanking it were a pad of yellow butter and a small container of syrup, ready to be drizzled. Next to the food was a paper cup filled with luke-warm water and a tea bag on a string ready to be dunked in the water. A curly black hair floated on top of the water. A gush of bile backed up in his throat. He replaced the cover over the uneaten food, his hand trembling slightly after the wave of nausea subsided.

In less than half an hour, a police officer returned and motioned Carl to the door to place his wrists in handcuffs. "We are taking you to the courthouse," said the polite officer.

"Are these really necessary?" asked Carl, lifting both arms and shaking the handcuffs. He felt the shame and humiliation creeping back. A flash of anxiety washed over him as the pain in his stomach returned. An involuntary deep sigh escaped from him as the police officer escorted him along the corridor, past the sleeping bodies of the other inmates in the adjacent jail cells.

"The handcuffs are part of the protocol," he replied. "I know in your case they are probably unnecessary, but we have to follow our normal procedures." He led Carl to a waiting cruiser and sat him in the back seat.

When Carl arrived at the small courthouse office, he found Martin waiting for him in a chair. Dressed in a black robe, he appeared prepared for the court. "You look like you had a rough night," he said.

Carl extended his hands towards the police officer, who removed the handcuffs from his wrists. He gently massaged his wrists, soothing the area where the metal rings from the cuffs had left their marks. "Not the kind of night I would like to re-live," replied Carl. "Do you think you can get me out of here?"

"I will do my best," said Martin. "In a few minutes, the court registrar will come and let us into the courthouse. You are to say nothing and let me do the talking. Much will depend on the position of the crown prosecutor and whether he has any objections to letting you out on bail. Either way, there is a good chance the judge will set bail at a high level. If that happens, you will have 48 hours to come up with the money. Do you have any questions?"

Before Carl could answer, there was a knock on the door. The door opened, and the man stated, "The court is ready for your hearing. Please, follow me."

The court registrar, a court official, escorted them into a courtroom that appeared vacant, save for a solitary woman. Carl surmised she was the court recorder. She possessed grey hair and worn facial features. Taking her place at a table positioned in front of where the judge would preside, she sported a set of black earphones. As she continued to type, she did not once lift her gaze from the screen of her laptop.

Carl took a seat next to Martin at the table and plopped down with a sigh. In walked another individual, donning a black robe that bore a striking resemblance to Martin's attire. He made his way over to the table on the other side of the room, where he sat down opposite Carl. Martin appeared to know the man as they waved to each other.

"All rise," said the court registrar. Carl and the others in the room stood. The judge, a woman in her 70s, walked in and sat in her chair behind the massive wooden desk.

"You may sit," said the court registrar. At the back of her head, the judge had her grey hair elegantly tied in a bun. Carl couldn't help but notice the stern expression etched on her face. *Just my luck. A woman judge. She is going to come down hard on me. I'll never get out of here.* His heart sank at the thought. Carl watched as she removed her laptop and placed it on the desk in front of her. She banged at the keys and then seemed to stop and look at the screen.

"This is a bail hearing," said the judge after a few minutes. "The charges are sexual assault and unwanted sexual touching. Mr. Wheeler? You are representing the defendant?"

Martin stood up. "Yes, your honour," he said. Martin cleared his throat. "Dr. Mackenzie is an upstanding member of the local community. He is a pillar of the surgical fraternity and is the current president of the Surgical Society. This is the first time he has been charged with any offense. There is no possibility of a flight risk as he plans to defend the charges vigorously. I ask that you grant him bail."

The judge banged away at the laptop while looking at Martin and then back at Carl. There was silence as she finished what she was typing. Her gaze shifted to the other man in the room.

"Mr. Jacobson, you are representing the crown?" asked the judge to the man opposite Carl.

"Yes, your honour," replied the crown attorney as he stood up. "This is a serious charge of sexual assault and unwanted sexual touching, but I have no objection to agreeing to bail if it is set at a high enough amount."

The judge stared at the crown attorney as her fingers continued to band away on the laptop. When she stopped typing, Carl saw her glance down at the screen and read what she had written. She appeared to think about what she was going to say before she looked up. "Bail is set at $100,000. Dr. Mackenzie, you must avoid contact with the complainant and you must surrender your passport to the court registrar. You have 48 hours to comply with the bail conditions. This court is adjourned."

Carl felt a wave of elation pass through him upon hearing the words from the judge. He could only think about getting home, having a hot shower, and then crashing out on his bed. He missed his kids and would be excited to see them when they came home from school at the end of the day. *I'll sort out the bail after I speak with my bank manager tomorrow.*

"You are free to leave," said Martin after the room had cleared. "Do you need a ride home?"

With a gesture of affirmation, Carl nodded. They made their way over to Martin's sleek Porsche Cayenne and climbed inside. The drive through the small town to Carl's house was quick and only took 10 minutes. Martin dropped him off and assured him they would have a conversation the following day. As Carl waved goodbye to him while he drove away, he couldn't help but feel an overwhelming sense of gratitude for finally being back home.

Following the traumatic experience of spending the night in jail, he experienced a profound sense of safety and security as he sauntered up to his house.

Carl took a few steps towards the front door, reached out his hand to grasp the doorknob, and carefully inserted the key into the lock. It wouldn't fit. He walked up to the keypad outside the garage and entered the code, feeling the cool metal buttons beneath his fingertips. Nothing happened. Carl attempted to use the house key to unlock the side door and gain access. The door stubbornly refused to budge, its lock holding tight. In a moment of despair, he sought refuge on the steps, sinking down and burying his face in his hands while tears streamed down his cheeks.

Chapter 10

"Let me get this right," said Melinda Pescone, the bank manager. She brushed her blonde locks away from her face. "You want to extend your line of credit another $600,000 to cover the bail and the anticipated legal fees?" She had concern written over her face as her brow furrowed. "The market value of your house at current prices, according to our charts, is...." She ran her finger to a point halfway down on the screen. "$1.3 million. You have a $200,000 mortgage, so we can easily extend a line of credit to another $600,000. We will usually allow 80% of the value of the house as a loan."

Carl breathed a sigh of relief. "Ok, thank you," he whispered. His eyes glanced at the paper he held in his hands. "Could you help me with the next step? I need to transfer $100,000 to the courts, and another $100,000 to Martin Wheeler, my lawyer." He handed her the banking information.

"I will get on it right away. You can tell them to expect to receive the transfers by tomorrow morning." Melinda looked at him as he stood up. "And Carl, you don't deserve this." She grasped his hand in hers. Her eyes glistened with tears. "This is so unfair. In my eyes, you will always be my hero with what you did to save my mother's life last year."

Carl felt emotion welling up inside of him. Until this last

issue arose, everyone he met except for Andrea thought he was an exceptional person. Now he was beginning to believe that Andrea was right and everyone else was wrong. He shook his head and muttered, "Thank you for your kindness, Melinda." But he didn't believe he deserved to be anyone's hero.

Just that morning, he had received a phone call from the past president of the Surgical Society asking him to step down from his duties as president. "Look," said Alister McGowan, "we go back a long way. Just step back until we clear up this mess. That's all I'm asking. We all support you here. Really..... we do. But we need to think of our members and how we can best represent them. Your unfortunate situation is causing too many distractions. We've had the press asking us how we feel about having a sexual.... well, you know what I mean. It is not a good reflection of our Surgical Society and our values if we keep you on at this delicate moment in your life."

"I'll send you my letter of resignation today," Carl told him, accepting that was the only workable solution.

Carl made his way to the Holiday Inn, a hotel where he had booked a room for $89 per night. Having provided care for his wife's hemorrhoids during the challenging delivery of their second child a few months ago, he had established a personal connection with the manager. He, too, was truly grateful for the surgical treatment Carl had provided when his wife needed it most.

Carl accessed his newly purchased laptop and logged into it. Andrea had locked all his possessions in the house. Despite many attempts, she refused to answer the phone. After he sent her a text, the only response she gave him was a message stating that she had taken the kids and requested him not to disturb her or attempt to find the children. She was pursuing a court order. She told him she would be successful at prohibiting him from gaining any form of access to them. In his message to Martin, he forwarded these communications and posed the question of what he should do regarding the passport surrender, now he could no longer access his house where he kept it.

"I'll speak with the judge. Don't worry about that for now," Martin replied with a text message.

Carl attempted to log on to the hospital website using his credentials. "Access denied. Contact the administrator," was the message that came up. Carl sighed and thought about what he should do. He called Fernando Rodriguez, the manager of informatics.

"Fernando," Carl said when he answered. "I can't access the hospital computer. Can you help me?" Fernando was quiet on the other end. "Fernando, are you there?"

"Carl," replied Fernando. "Barry Little, your chief of staff asked me to remove your access until you have sorted out your problems."

Carl's heart skipped a beat, and he felt faint as he hung up the phone. The entire hospital and town now knew about what happened. He wished the judge had denied him bail so he wouldn't have to face anyone he ran into. The embarrassment and shame overwhelmed him. *How much worse could things get?*

His phone rang. It was Michael Smithers, the lawyer assigned to him from the Medical Protective Agency. "There is an emergency hearing at the hospital this evening at the Medical Advisory Committee to determine whether you should undergo midterm suspension. They have invited you to attend by Zoom."

"Oh my God," whispered Carl. "This is getting worse by the hour for me." The feeling of suffocation overwhelmed him, making it seem like he couldn't breathe. With the tightness in his chest, he found himself taking short, intermittent breaths. A feeling of dizziness overcame him. It didn't feel right for him to be judged by his colleagues at a time when he was feeling so vulnerable. "Can't we delay this?"

"You sound like you are having difficulty breathing. Are you OK?"

Carl knew he had to calm down. He took a few deep breaths and said, "Sorry. It is such a shock. I'm not sure I am ready for this."

"The hearing will go ahead with or without you. You will have the opportunity to speak and you can tell them what happened and how you feel about everything, or you can say nothing. As your lawyer, I will not have the opportunity to say anything and can only observe. They may ask you some questions. When they finish, they will ask us to leave. They will deliberate and then they might invite us back for more discussion, or they might send us a registered letter within 24 hours telling us their decision. I would suggest you think about what you wish to say." Michael paused as if he were choosing his next words carefully. "Your story sounds innocent enough to me, so my advice would be to tell them the truth about what happened and hopefully, calmer heads will prevail."

"Ok," replied Carl. "See you in 2 hours."

The next 2 hours passed slowly for Carl. He knew he had to remain calm and avoid losing it like he had done when he had met with Barry a few days ago. That HR lawyer, Stephanie, really upset him with her condescending attitude. He hoped she wouldn't be there tonight. He rehearsed what he wanted to say and made a few notes so he wouldn't forget the important points. When the time rolled around to log into Zoom, he felt he was ready.

Carl took a deep breath and logged in. Zoom immediately placed him in the waiting room with a notice that they would admit to the meeting him shortly. After 30 seconds, the Medical Advisory

Committee view of the meeting opened on his screen. Barry Little, along with all the chiefs of the departments, sat around an oblong wooden table, each with a small pile of papers in front of them. Carl noted the CEO and vice presidents were sitting in a row of chairs along the window. Beside them sat Stephanie. His heart skipped a beat and felt like it plummeted into his boots.

"Hi Carl," said Barry. "Thank you for coming. We are here tonight to determine whether we should deliver a mid-term suspension to you. Is there anything you would like to tell us about what happened?"

"Thank you for the opportunity to speak," Carl replied. "I'll tell you what happened and you can see for yourselves that this has been a colossal mistake of epic proportions." Carl then recounted the story of what had happened. 30 minutes later, after finishing, he asked, "Does anyone have any questions?" The room remained silent.

Barry glanced around the room. "It seems like no one has questions, so you are free to sign off so we can deliberate. Thank you for your explanation of what happened. We will let you know the outcome as soon as possible."

Carl logged out. Within 30 seconds, his phone chirped. It was Michael. "You did great tonight, Carl," he said. "You were calm, cogent and put together some very persuasive arguments. I think this will turn out in our favour. I watched the faces of your colleagues. They seemed sympathetic, and many nodded when you told them you had done nothing wrong."

"I'm a little worried about the HR lawyer, Stephanie," answered Carl. "She had a meltdown on me when I was in Barry's office a few days ago."

"She has no voting rights, just the chief of departments can vote. The chief of staff only gets to vote to break a tie. I think we will be OK."

"Thanks for the encouragement," said Carl, as he yawned, realizing how tired he was. "I think I'll go to bed now." They agreed to talk in the morning. He felt himself drift off to a dreamless sleep in less than a minute. His last thought as he drifted off was that things were finally turning around for him. *I'm going to get my life back, and this is just the start.*

The ringing of his cell phone awoke Carl. He glanced at the time. It was 2 a.m. Michael was on the line. "They voted to suspend your hospital privileges."

Chapter 11

"We've shared laughter, tears, triumphs, and setbacks—a lifetime of memories," Andy Appleby, Carl's longtime childhood friend, reflected, a wistful smile gracing his lips. "You can be certain I will be here for you and that I would never abandon you. Let's not forget all those crazy times we had as teenagers, constantly finding ourselves in trouble and having to bail each other out of predicaments."

A smile touched Carl's lips, a genuine smile, the first one he could recall experiencing in what felt like an eternity, a full seven days. Andy was right. They were inseparable, practically joined at the hip, and they consistently surprised each other with spontaneous acts of helpfulness and support, each one always there to aid the other.

Thirteen-year-old Andy, feeling adventurous, had taken his mother's Volkswagen Beetle for an unauthorized joyride. The time was well past midnight when the ringing of the telephone startled Carl from his slumber, bringing with it an urgent message. With a panicked cry into his cellphone, Andy exclaimed, "I'm in deep shit and I don't know what to do! I am out of gas. My mom is going to kill me."

Carl, always the cool one in a time of crisis, even at a young age, said, "Where are you?"

"Exhibition Park near the wading pool," replied Andy.

"Ok," said Carl after a moment of thought. "Here's what we are going to do." Carl told Andy the plan.

Within the next fifteen minutes, Carl was pouring gas into the Beetle. "I took the lawnmower's gas container from the garage and put it in my backpack. Because the streets were empty, the bicycle ride was very easy."

"Thanks Carl," shouted Andy as he drove away. "You saved my life!" Driving his mother's beloved Beetle toward his home, Carl watched as Andy carefully engaged the gear, anticipating the smooth shifts. Carl followed him home on his bike as they lived two houses apart. He watched as Andy parked it on the street directly in front of their house in its usual and customary parking spot.

Even after all these years, his mother is still in the dark and oblivious to the details of Andy's mischievous adventure. That marked the beginning of their mutual reliance and interconnectedness, a dependence that would shape their futures in profound ways. Having shared an apartment during their undergraduate years at university, they remained close friends throughout their lives.

"Remember Betty Boop? Grade 12?" asked Andy, bringing Carl back to the present. "I remember feeling her breasts while we were necking in my dad's Ford Escalade. She kept on pushing my hand away, but she wanted to keep kissing me. I kept trying to touch her, though, like any normal hormone ravaged adolescent. Talk about getting a mixed message. I could have been in the same spot you are in now. In fact, 100% of males have done the exact same thing as you. That's why this is so crazy and why you have to fight it."

Carl thought about this before he spoke. "There are two main issues I am told by my lawyer that will be problematic for me. The first issue is that of consent. Imagine if a man is walking down the street and grabs a woman's breast. Most people would consider that sexual assault. Unwanted sexual touching. Let's say you are kissing Betty Boop in grade 12 and she doesn't want you to touch her breasts, but you do anyway. That is unwanted sexual touching and in the eyes of the law, it is the same thing as in the first example."

Reaching down, Carl grasped the frosty glass of beer that was waiting for him and took a deep swallow. As they talked, they sat in the Baker Street Station pub, in the town center of Guelph, enjoying the atmosphere and each other's company. The din from other patron's conversations and the clanking of dishes from the kitchen kept their conversation private.

"The second issue of significant concern is the inherent power imbalance that exists between individuals occupying differing professional roles, specifically, a surgeon and a floor cleaner. That distinction raises the bar substantially, making it considerably more difficult to obtain truly informed consent. In actuality, the hospital maintains a strict policy explicitly forbidding any form of fraternization between individuals where a power differential exists, ensuring a professional and ethical work environment. Hospital policy requires the human resources department to assess and verify that suitable workplace safety measures and protocols are in place and are being followed. Because that did not happen in my situation, the absence of consent in touching Sabrina's breast becomes a significantly more serious and difficult issue to justify."

Andy looked at Carl with his mouth agape. "There is every reason to believe that those who possess sound judgment and rational thought will ultimately succeed in exonerating you," he replied. "The hospital and the College of Physicians and Surgeons have suspended your surgical privileges, which unfortunately prevents you from earning an income. Following a request from your colleagues, they asked you to step down from your presidential role within the surgical society. Access to your house is currently unavailable to you for reasons outside of your control. You haven't even had a trial yet, and they have mercilessly judged and severely punished you! Whatever happened to the principle of innocent until proven guilty, a cornerstone of our justice system?"

Carl looked at his friend with sadness. "The '#MeToo'

movement," Carl explained while shaking his head, "presents yet another significant obstacle to my pursuit of a fair trial, joining the several other impediments. The courts have a long history of dismissing sexual assault complaints by using victim-blaming language, such as the statement, 'she was asking for it by getting in the car alone with the guy,' or, 'she was kissing him and obviously there was implied consent.' This is a deeply problematic and an unacceptable way to treat survivors of sexual assault. When the courts review the current legislation, the direction is clear. A lack of consent results in a ruling that invariably favours the plaintiff."

Andy's expression was of astonishment. "Tell them it never happened. Tell them you didn't touch her breast, and she is lying."

Carl laughed while shaking his head. "I can't do that, Andy. I touched her breast because I thought that was what she wanted. That the situation could be misconstrued as a sexual assault charge is a testament to how distorted things have become. The weight of this unjust charge has crushed me, and my only solace is the possibility of a favorable judgment. With a little effort, I could return to my position at the hospital. Once the sexual assault charge is no longer a factor, I'll have the opportunity to repair my life and reconnect with my children, free of Andrea's manipulative hold."

"It seems so unfair," sighed Andy.

"In our capacity as doctors, they hold us to a higher standard of accountability than that which is expected of the average person. Accountants, including yourself, are subject to the same heightened level of responsibility and scrutiny in handling financial resources. They would expect you to adhere to principles and standards of conduct that the rest of us, frankly, are not expected to know or follow. In the same vein, the legal system and laws of the country also operate under this same principle. Because a position of trust, such as working as a doctor, requires a high level of integrity, even a seemingly minor infraction can be viewed as a serious breach."

They both sat in silence as they thought about all this. "I understand you'd prefer not to receive money, but I insist on helping you out, even if it's just a little."

Carl shook his head. "I can never do that, Andy. I feel incredibly fortunate to have you in my corner; your presence alone is enough to give me strength and confidence. With a heavy heart, I am making preparations for a court decision that I expect will be disappointing and not in my favour. I find it incredibly difficult to process the magnitude of everything that has occurred."

"Well, no matter the outcome, we will get through this together. Our lives have always intertwined," said Andy. "I don't need to tell you this, but I will anyway. Consistent with our history, the closing of one avenue always heralds the opening of another. A fresh path always appearing when an old one is closed."

"It's hard for me to see how any good can ever come of this," said Carl as he felt his eyes moisten. "One thing I am learning, though, is how to find gratitude. The alternative is to get consumed with bitterness and anger. I battle these opposing forces every day. Having you as a friend gives me gratitude."

The two friends embraced wordlessly, both quietly sobbing.

Chapter 12

"It's important we push for a speedy trial, so the judge sees you are determined to clear your name," Martin had told him after he had received the first instalment of $100,000. Carl was able to funnel another $200,000 to Martin before Andrea had frozen their joint bank account so she could preserve her half of the value of the house. Carl still owed him $200,000. Martin had wanted payment before the trial had started, but Carl could not come up with the funds.

"When they release the $100,000 bail after the trial, you can use that money," Carl suggested when they met to discuss payment. "The remaining amount I owe you....well, I'll have to come up with a plan to pay the rest."

"Where are you living now?" asked Martin. They sat in Martin's office on the 47th floor in downtown Toronto. They could see the cityscape stretching out before them, and the brilliant blue reflection of Lake Ontario. The thick, brightly coloured carpet and solid oak wainscotting in the lawyer's office made him acutely aware of the vast difference between his current living situation.

Inside the small room Carl had rented, which measured 10 feet by 10 feet, his first sight of a single bed that filled the room against a wall with yellow wallpaper that was peeling off sank his spirits. The bedsheets were so thin that the springs of the mattress poked through. Once every 2 weeks, the landlord scheduled the sheets a thorough washing, but it didn't seem to eliminate the dirt or odours. Standing in one corner was a small white porcelain sink, its cracked surface reflecting the room's soft glow. The drain in the sink was a rusty orange color, with stubborn stains that refused to come off. The floors, once resembling wood, were now worn down to bare plywood in most areas, revealing their true nature as vinyl tiles. Despite being labelled as a nonsmoking room, the unmistakable combination of stale cigarettes and bleach permeated the air.

The five men who occupied the rooms on that floor shared the bathroom at the end of the hall, with its worn-out, chipped ceramic tiles and flickering fluorescent lights. Often, the residents had to deal with the constant frustration of a frequently clogged toilet and the perpetual absence of toilet paper. The $800 per month rent charged by his landlord left only $220 for food. The landlord allowed Carl to have a shower once a week in the basement. In the rooming house, there were 25 men who followed a schedule to use the shower, with each person given a 30-minute slot. His shower day was every Thursday between 7 p.m. and 7:30 pm.

Carl sighed. "I was lucky to find a place, but that takes most of my unemployment cheque. Still, it was that or the homeless shelter on Main Street. Andrea transferred all of our joint account money into her account. She maxed out my Visa card, so it doesn't work any longer. I have no money."

Martin looked at him with concern. "It should all be over soon. You have already pleaded not guilty at the preliminary hearing. Tomorrow, the trial will start. It should take no longer than 2 days as there will be only 3 witnesses, including yourself. I will ask you to testify on the second day. With any luck, the judge will make a ruling quickly and you can get on with your life. Do you have any questions?"

Carl glanced at Martin, then shook his head. Martin said, "we'll see you tomorrow morning at the courthouse then."

Carl got up to leave. Martin walked him to the elevator. They arrived as the elevator door opened and he reached into his pocket and pulled out his wallet. He carefully peeled off two $20 bills. "Take this and buy yourself dinner."

Carl's gaze fell upon of money, his eyes fixed on the notes. A sense of shame and embarrassment overcame him as he pondered whether to take the money. For the past two months, he had been experiencing a persistent sense of helplessness, but thanks to the help of Ray, his psychiatrist, he could come to terms with the fact that there were certain things happening in his life that were beyond his control. He felt a surge of relief knowing the provincial health plan covered his psychiatric treatment; the financial burden was one less thing to worry about. Every week, they would meet, and he would provide invaluable support. He had advised him to identify the moments where he held some level of control, and subsequently make a decision that aligns with his deeply ingrained values, a decision he can confidently live with.

This was one of those moments. He would rather go hungry than take the money Martin had offered him. Carl entered the elevator and pushed the ground floor button, saying nothing. When the doors closed, he took 3 deep breaths and smiled. *I still have some control over my life.*

****

"All rise," shouted the court registrar. Carl stood up with the rest of the people in the courthouse. The same graying 70-year-old judge that had granted him bail was presiding. As she walked, her black robe billowed and swayed with each step. It was only after she settled herself behind the wooden desk when the court registrar signalled it was permissible that the rest of the people in the room could take their seats. It had been 2 months since he had been out on bail. This was the day 1 of the trial.

Carl quickly glanced over at the crowd that was seated in the visitor's section. He noticed Stephanie Laurenson, the lawyer from the hospital, who would also serve as one of the witnesses. For a moment, their gazes met and locked before she averted her eyes. Occupying the front row was a reporter from the local newspaper, attentively taking notes. With a smile directed at Carl, she subtly conveyed that she was firmly supporting him. He recognized a couple of women working as cleaning staff at the hospital. His closest friend from university, Andy Appleby, was waving at him from deep in the middle of the crowd. He gave him a thumbs up as if to say, you can do this, Carl. Most of the audience he did not recognize. Carl turned to face forward and looked over at the crown prosecutor.

"Your witness, Ms. Patel," said the judge to the crown prosecutor. The woman who was sitting at the desk next to Carl's stood up. Taking a moment to straighten her black robe, she stood up, ensuring it fell perfectly. With her face beautifully framed by her short dark hair, she wore large fashionable blue glasses that covered her striking blue eyes. Her diminutive stature belied her powerful presence, as her voice resonated with authority in the court chambers.

"The crown calls Sabrina Hawryluk," she said with authority.

Martin leaned across and whispered in Carl's ear. "Instead of being physically present, she will give her testimony through a Zoom video call. To facilitate the process for victims of sexual assault, the courts have introduced changes aimed at encouraging them to come forward with their stories. It was only a few minutes ago when I heard about this in the judge's chambers."

The sight of Sabrina's face on the TV screens, placed at the front of the court, captured everyone's attention. Carl's heart skipped a beat as he saw her for the first time since the incident happened. She was wearing a white turtle-neck sweater. Which covered her slender neck. She had tied her blonde hair chastely in a bun at the back of her head. Her eyes cast downward, focused on the screen in front of her, betrayed no emotion. Carl took three deep breaths and could feel his racing heart slow down. *Why is it, after all the grief she has inflicted upon me, I still find her so attractive?*

At the side of the witness stand, Ms. Patel sat facing the judge where they had positioned a laptop, ready to ask questions to Sabrina. "Good morning, Sabrina," said Ms. Patel. "Thank you for joining us virtually through Zoom. You will only see and hear me in the room until my friend Martin Wheeler joins and begins asking questions after I finish. Just so you know, in the legal profession, it is customary for lawyers to address each other as 'my friend' as a way to uphold a sense of civility. The others in the room can see and hear you, but you cannot see them. Do you have questions about that?"

"No questions," said Sabrina.

"Perhaps you could tell us what happened," suggested Ms. Patel.

Sabrina told a story very similar to the one Carl had

recounted, except for omitting the parts where she asked him to kiss her. After she had finished, Ms. Patel said, "Thank you for coming forward with this. I know it has been difficult for you. I'm going to ask you a few questions. At any time did you give Dr. Mackenzie permission to touch your breast?"

"No," answered Sabrina.

"Did you ever suggest to Dr. Mackenzie you wished to partake in a sexual relationship with him?"

Again, Sabrina answered, "no."

"Why were you kissing him in his car, then?"

"The impression I had was that the kiss was a friendly goodnight gesture, resembling the sort of embrace that occurs when two individuals unexpectedly meet after a long absence on the street."

"When he touched your breast, was that something you wanted him to do?"

Sabrina answered the question quickly. "No."

Ms. Patel glanced at the judge and said, "no more questions, your honour."

The judge looked over at Michael and asked, "do you wish to question the witness?"

"Yes, your honour," replied Michael. Making a deliberate move, he got up from his chair and positioned himself purposefully in front of the laptop, ensuring that Sabrina had a perfect line of sight for him. Carl's eyes fixated on Sabrina's image, hoping to catch a glimpse of her reaction, yet her face remained completely void of any emotion.

"Until the incident you described, did Dr. Mackenzie ever make any suggestive sexual comments to you?" asked Michael.

"No," answered Sabrina.

"Until the incident, did Dr. Mackenzie ever touch you in a sexual manner?"

"No."

"Until the incident, did Dr. Mackenzie always treat you with respect and dignity?"

"Yes."

"No more questions, your honour." Michael sauntered back to his chair and sat down next to Carl. Carl felt confused by the brevity of the questions. He glanced at Michael and was about to say something when the judge announced, "I think we will take a break for lunch before the next witness."

As the judge exited the room, the court registrar requested everyone to stand, and they all complied. Carl turned, trying to keep his anger in check, and asked Michael, "Why didn't you ask her to tell the truth about the kissing part?"

Michael turned to Carl and replied, "Let me take you to lunch and I'll review the strategy, then." Michael turned on his heels and rushed out of the courthouse, with Carl trailing closely behind.

Chapter 13

The club sandwich Carl had ordered for lunch tasted salty and had too much mayonnaise. He could feel the heartburn beginning after only a few bites and he put the sandwich down. Several swallows of carbonated water helped, but the pain in his chest from the reflux of acid into his esophagus persisted. He reached into his pocket and found several Gaviscon tablets. He chewed them, which gave him some relief that he knew would only be temporary.

"Sabrina came across as a reliable witness," said Martin. "Asking her to change her story would have only infuriated the crown prosecutor and the judge. Treating her with the same respect and dignity you have always done sends a clear message to them that you have integrity and honesty. When you get the opportunity to tell the story from your side, we will have the advantage because of the respectful way we handled Sabrina with our questions."

Carl nodded and said, "It comes down to credibility, doesn't it? You are saying that if we pave the pathway forward with respectability and credibility, the judge will have no choice but to cast doubt on her story and believe mine?"

With a single nod, Martin conveyed his agreement. He had just shoveled a forkful of Caesar salad into his mouth, so he couldn't speak. Carl took a quick glance at his unappetizing lunch and immediately lost his appetite. Based on Martin's recommendation, he had ordered what was supposed to be the house specialty, only to realize he had made the wrong choice. The legal strategy described by Michael left Carl feeling uncertain, as he pondered its potential flaws. Women dominated these proceedings, with the judge, the crown prosecutor, and now Stephanie taking charge. The way women perceive the world in relation to sexual assault has always differed from men. It never occurred to Carl that touching a woman's breast during intimacy without her explicit verbal consent could be sexual assault. *The next step will require a signed written consent. Talk about throwing cold water on intimacy....*

With lunch over, they walked back to the courthouse. The court registrar followed the same routine when the judge entered the room, and the crown prosecutor called Stephanie Laurenson to the witness stand.

"The day following the incident," said Stephanie, "Sabrina came to the HR department to speak with me. She asked for time off for mental health reasons. When I delved into her story a little more, she reluctantly described the incident. I had little choice but to ask her to file a police report as the law had been broken and a sexual assault had occurred. The hospital has strict policies that Dr. Mackenzie would have known about that prohibit relationships between staff as there will be a power differential. People perceive a doctor as authoritative, while someone like Sabrina, a floor cleaner, is seen as susceptible to that person in authority."

Stephanie took a sip of water before she continued. "For the past 6 months, I have been monitoring the sexually inappropriate comments that some staff in the operating room have been complaining about. The CEO has tasked me to put an end to this unprofessional workplace practice. Even though many in the operating room, including doctors and nurses, take part in this unprofessional behavior, it is ultimately the surgeon's responsibility to intervene and end it. Dr. MacKenzie's operating room was the setting for the latest incident, adding to the growing list of unsettling events on...." Stephanie paused and her brow furrowed as she appeared to recollect the exact date. "On December 2nd, of last year, when Dr. Mackenzie's patient, an orthopedic surgeon, had a routine appendectomy. Bandages were carefully applied to his scrotum, creating the illusion of a vasectomy, while his toenails were painted a vibrant shade of pink. The behavior was not only unprofessional but also crossed the line into sexual misconduct. Some sexually explicit remarks were exchanged during that operation, and Dr. Mackenzie had a chance to intervene but chose not to."

Carl couldn't believe what he was hearing. His lunchtime heartburn had returned with a vengeance. Retrieving a handful of antacid tablets from his pocket, he began chewing on them. He leaned over and whispered into Martin's ear. "What the fuck is going on? How is she allowed to say those things?"

Martin shot to his feet. "Objection, your honour. The charges against my client have no connection to the work of Ms. Laurenson in managing behavior in the operating room. This is highly prejudicial and irrelevant. I kindly request that you retract her testimony."

Ms. Patel stood up. The judge acknowledged her and said, "Ms. Patel? You wish to respond?"

"This goes to the heart of the culture that led to the sexual assault, your honour," she began. "In an environment where they allow such inappropriate activity, it is understandable how this becomes acceptable workplace behavior where no boundaries are established, and a sexual assault results. The power differential became firmly entrenched and played a role in why the incident occurred."

Martin shot to his feet. "Your honour..."

"Sit down, Mr. Wheeler," she commanded. She glared at him, pausing as if to establish she was the one in charge, not him. "I've heard what you have to say. I'm going to take a 15-minute break and then make a ruling about whether to accept this testimony." She stood up and exited with the court registrar announcing the others in the room to stand as well.

Carl entered the washroom and immediately headed for the toilet stall, the scent of disinfectant lingering in the air. He doubled over the toilet bowl, heaving as his stomach forcefully expelled the small amount of food he had consumed for lunch. His body broke out in a clammy, cold sweat, prompting him to hastily splash cold water on his face, trying to alleviate the perspiration on his brow. Staring back at him in the mirror was a thin face, haggard from the 15-pound weight loss, with a beard that had once been stylish but now appeared unkempt. His mind wandered to the advice his psychiatrist had given him about accepting things that were beyond his control.

"Getting wound up about what happens in the courtroom will only add to your free-floating anxiety," Ray had told him. "The tsunami is coming, and you have done whatever you could to protect yourself. If it lifts you up and carries you off, surrender to the force and let it guide you. Once the water level recedes, you'll find yourself in a much better place than if you had struggled to swim against the current."

The judge returned to the courtroom a few minutes after Carl had entered. He felt better having expelled the toxic remnants of his lunch. He also felt better after thinking about the wisdom in the advice Ray had given him. This was an arduous journey he was travelling, and he needed all the help he could get to guide him.

"I've made my decision," said the judge. She paused as if to give the impression she had considered both arguments equally before arriving at her conclusion. "I'm going to allow Ms. Laurenson's testimony.

To his surprise, Carl did not feel the expected pain in his abdomen or experience the usual shortness of breath that followed such a detrimental ruling. His breathing remained regular, and his pulse remained stable. *The tsunami has arrived. I am in control. I am going to go with the flow. It will allow me to arrive at a better place than if I try to fight something I have no control over.*

Chapter 14

The next day, Carl stood before the court and gave his testimony. It surprised him that the crown prosecutor treated him with a similar courtesy as Martin had done with Sabrina with her questions. He took advantage of the opportunity to once again emphasize the innocent nature of the encounter, while also emphasizing the intense passion he felt when she kissed him. "I thought that was what she wanted. My intention was never to cause her harm or hurt her. I deeply and sincerely regret the actions that occurred on that day, and if I had the chance to go back in time, I would definitely choose to act differently."

"You did very well," said Martin as Carl sat beside him at the defence table. "As you gave your testimony, I watched the judge and noticed a gentle compassion in her eyes, as if she genuinely empathized with and trusted your account."

"Thank you," said Carl. He had the feeling of hopefulness for the first time in the past few days. There were no more witnesses, and the final arguments would begin shortly. Ms. Patel would go first, followed by Martin.

Ms. Patel stood to address the judge. She left her papers at her table so she could walk around the room if she needed to. "Your honour, both the victim and the defence have presented strikingly similar accounts of the incident. Dr. Mackenzie is a respected member of the community and has suffered a great deal already because of his actions that evening in December. But both you and I know we have a responsibility to maintain the integrity of the law. Engaging in any form of unwanted physical contact, specifically touching someone's breast without their consent, is a serious criminal offense. It is sexual assault. There is no gray area here. Dr. Mackenzie broke the law and must face the consequences. The responsibility lies with you to find him guilty and impose a minimum prison sentence of 1 year as punishment. Thank you, your honour."

Carl had expected what Ms. Patel would say. Martin had briefed him and was almost spot on with the words she would use. Still, Carl felt his heart miss a beat when she summarized to the judge by saying he should go to jail. It was different knowing what someone would say than hearing the words resonate off the walls of the courtroom. He looked straight ahead and tried to hide his disappointment, following the instructions Martin had given him that morning.

Martin stood to address the judge. "Your honour. The stories about what happened that night are indeed very similar, as my friend has astutely observed. Sabrina failed to mention that she was the instigator of the encounter, which changes the entire perspective of the story. Sabrina boldly asked him to kiss her, and she eagerly pulled him closer, pressing their lips together tightly. It was her who initiated the passionate exchange, pressing her tongue inside his mouth. This was not a casual, friendly peck on the cheek. It was a lingering, passionate kiss that spoke volumes. This was the invitation she was giving him for intimacy and to touch her breasts. Intimate encounters often rely heavily on nonverbal cues. Every day, in cities around the world, this scene unfolds thousands of times, with countless encounters happening. Just think about the overwhelming burden we would face if every single one of those encounters ended up in court."

In a gesture filled with sadness, Martin walked around the front of the defence table and pointed directly at Carl while shaking his head. As if he himself was the one feeling remorse, he glanced down at the floor. "Dr. Mackenzie's remorse is undeniable, having clearly misinterpreted Sabrina's intentions, as you have heard. Since losing his position at the hospital, he has endured immeasurable suffering. With his wife having left him and having no contact with his children for over 2 months, he felt a profound sense of loss and longing. In the rooming house, his living quarters comprise a compact 10-foot by 10-foot room, where he spends most of his time. Having lost everything, he now relies on social assistance to make ends meet. The punishment he has endured has been far more severe than confinement behind bars. The only fair judgement is to find him not guilty, allowing him to start rebuilding his shattered life. Thank you, your honour."

Martin took a seat beside Carl. Martin's words ceased reverberating from the walls, leaving the room in silence. The impact of his words seemed to resonate within each person in the room, as if they had become a part of their being. The judge's gaze shifted from Carl to Martin and finally landed on Ms. Patel. It was only after about 30 seconds that the judge cleared her throat and said, "Thank you, counsellors. I will have my decision sometime within the coming week, possibly as early as tomorrow. This court is adjourned."

"All rise," said the court registrar for the last time.

****

The sound of Carl's phone ringing broke the silence in the room. In the rooming house, he sat on his bed, feeling the worn-out mattress beneath him. The cramped room left him with nowhere else to sit. Thoughts of the past 2 days flooded his mind, creating a whirlwind of memories. Although he could do nothing about what had unfolded during the trial, the scenes continued to replay in his mind. It was a welcome distraction to answer the phone.

"The judge has arrived at her decision," said Martin.

"That was fast, after less than 24 hours." replied Carl. "Is that a good thing or a bad thing?"

"Hard to tell, but meet me at the courthouse conference room at 12:45 and we'll run through a few things before court starts at 1 p.m."

Martin and Carl sat in the conference room across from each other. "We have to be ready for all the scenarios," Martin said. "The judge may side with us and find you not guilty. Obviously, that would be the best decision and you would get back to as close to your former life as possible."

"What's the chance of that happening?" asked Carl.

"I think it is a good chance the judge will side in our favour. There have been many cases similar where the ruling has been in favour of the defendant when sexual assault has been alleged, but the judge found it was consensual touching that occurred. We made a good argument for that."

"What are the other scenarios?"

"If the judge finds you guilty, the worst scenario would be jail time, but that is extremely unlikely to happen, given the circumstances of what transpired. A guilty verdict would most likely result in a suspended sentence, which means no jail, but you would have a criminal record."

There was a knock on the door. The court registrar poked his head into the room and said, "The judge is ready to convene."

Carl could feel his pulse racing and the familiar pain in his abdomen when the free-floating anxiety set in as he walked towards the courtroom and sat in his usual seat. Ms. Patel was already there and was banging on her laptop. She did not look up when he arrived. He took 3 deep breaths and tried to think about what Ray would tell him to think about if he could whisper in his ear with advice. Nothing came to mind.

"All rise," said the court registrar. Carl was deep in thought when the sudden words startled him, causing him to jump up. With each passing second, Carl's uneasiness grew more palpable, knowing that this dreaded moment was finally upon him. After just a few words from the judge, his future would be determined. The judge entered the room with a confident stride and settled into her familiar chair, ready to preside over the proceedings.

"Thank you for coming back so quickly," she said. "The crown and defence both requested a speedy trial, and I want to express my gratitude to both parties for that. My decision was a difficult one. The law explicitly states that unsolicited touching of the breast is sexual assault. On the other hand, during an intimate encounter, the act of touching often happens without explicit verbal consent, relying on what is commonly known as implied consent."

The judge paused and looked at her papers. "In this case, the law is clear. The act of touching the breast without consent took place, and based on the defined criteria, it can be classified as a case of sexual assault. From the evidence presented, I have reached the verdict of guilty against Dr. Mackenzie for the charge of sexual assault. As a consequence, I hereby sentence him to a six-month suspended sentence. For a period of ten years, he will remain on the provincial sexual offender registry, and if there are no further incidents, his name may be eligible for removal. I will ensure that my complete report is ready for distribution in a maximum of 14 days. Dr. Mackenzie, you must report immediately to the court registrar. This court is adjourned."

As the courtroom emptied, Carl remained seated, his expression frozen in stunned silence. He remained completely still, not even a twitch. Deep down, he had always known this would be the outcome, even though he had hoped for a different result. He had hit rock bottom, feeling the weight of despair pressing down on him. He had reached the bottom with no other place to land. Martin explained the concept and workings of a six-month suspended sentence to him, but his words failed to resonate with him. He observed Martin's lips moving and heard him speaking, but none of his words were comprehensible. The room began to spin, and a veil of darkness descended over his eyes. As he fell off his chair, he could feel the sudden rush of gravity pulling him towards the floor.

Then he felt nothing.

Chapter 15

Carl woke up in unfamiliar surroundings. He could hear the rhythmic sound of monitors, his own heartbeat reflected on the pulse oximeter. He glanced up at the monitors. The EKG was regular, the heart rate was 80, and the blood pressure was 124/78.

"You're awake," said a voice coming from the doorway. "I'm Gladys, your nurse. How are you feeling?"

"Where am I?" asked Carl.

"You are in the hospital," replied Gladys. "You fainted in the courthouse and hit your head. The doctor thinks you might have a concussion. The CAT scan was OK from this afternoon, though. Do you have a headache?"

Carl glanced up at her and said, "I feel fine, just a little tired. How long do I have to stay here?"

"We'll see how you feel in the morning. Perhaps the doctor will discharge you then."

Carl sat on the edge of the bed. An intravenous line hung from his left arm. A nurse or technician had attached a blood pressure cuff to his right arm, programming it to cycle every 10 minutes. The last blood pressure recorded was on the monitor. "I want to leave now," said Carl.

"Ahhh," said the nurse. "That would not be a good idea. We

would like to keep an eye on you until at least the morning to make sure you are OK."

Carl stood up. "I need to go to the bathroom. Could you disconnect me from all this stuff?"

Gladys walked to the bedside and disconnected the BP cuff, pulse oximeter, and EKG leads. Carl wheeled the IV pole into the bathroom and shut the door. When he finished and walked to his bed, he could hear two people arguing in the hallway. He paused so he could listen.

"I told you not to go into the room by yourself," Carl heard one voice say. "He is a known sexual offender. It's all over the news. Next time, call security and they can accompany you."

"That's crazy," said the voice belonging to Gladys. "He's harmless. Besides, he used to work here as a surgeon. Everyone knows him. Some even say that they unfairly accused him."

"I am in charge of the floor," said the first voice. "I will have to remove you from your position if you do not follow our protocol for convicted felons."

"That's bullshit," said Gladys, her footsteps echoed in the hallway as she stormed away.

Carl sat on the bed and placed his head in his hands. *So, this is how it is going to be. This has got to be the worst day of my life. I feel so humiliated. I do not think I can take much more.* He could feel tears well up as a jolt of anxiety ran through his body, bringing the accompanying abdominal pain. He struggled to catch his breath, his chest constricting with pain. *Is the tightness in my chest and the sharp pain shooting down my left arm indicative of a heart attack?* Feeling faint, he collapsed onto the bed and stared up at the ceiling. He closed his eyes and focused on his breath, taking three deliberate, unhurried inhales and exhales. With each passing moment, the chest tightness lessened, and the faintness subsided completely.

Carl glanced at the intravenous, its clear liquid slowly dripping into his veins. *I need to get out of here.* Carl reached over and shut off the IV, then swiftly withdrew the IV catheter from his arm. To stop the bleeding, he gently pressed a tissue against the site. Tucked away beneath his bed, he found his bag of clothing and his cellphone within easy reach. He hurriedly threw on his clothes and swiftly left the hospital room. Next door, there was a fire exit that provided a convenient and discreet way to leave the ward without triggering any alarms.

Right next to the hospital entrance, there was a spacious main lobby filled with inviting, cozy chairs. As he sat down, he could hear the distant sound of cars passing by, while he hailed an Uber to take him back to his rooming house. The TV was blaring, filling the room with a loud, obnoxious noise. "Just in," stated the announcer, his voice echoing through the room. "Today, Dr. Carl

MacKenzie, the disgraced local surgeon, received a six-month suspended sentence and will be required to register as a sexual offender for the next decade." Carl glanced at the TV to see his face plastered over the screen.

An 8-year-old boy who had stopped kicking the soccer ball he was playing with to watch the TV pointed to Carl and yelled. "There he is! The man on TV!"

The mother rushed over and grabbed her son's hand. She stared directly at Carl as she whisked past and whispered, "Stay away from my son, you pervert."

Carl stared back at them incredulously. *It is only getting worse.*

****

Back at the rooming house, Carl secured his door with a click and collapsed onto his bed, the exhaustion settling into his bones. The anxiety he continued to experience was overwhelming, reaching unprecedented levels. He tried pacing on the cramped floor, taking only three steps before having to abruptly turn around. Suddenly, a sharp pain shot through his lower abdomen. He doubled over. Realizing the urgency of the situation, he knew he had a limited window of approximately 30 seconds to reach the restroom at the far end of the hallway, before an unfortunate accident occurred. As he hurriedly made his way down the hallway, his sole aim was to reach the bathroom, but to his dismay, he discovered someone was using it. Upon hearing the knock, a gruff reply responded, "I'll be out shortly after finishing up."

Carl anxiously paced back and forth in front of the restroom, feeling the intense cramps growing stronger. As the door creaked open, he felt a rush of relief wash over him and his eyes widened as a man of immense size emerged from behind it. He fixed his gaze on Carl, as if he couldn't tear his eyes away. "You, of all people, the pervert! You have the audacity to interrupt me while I am trying to fulfil my duties. I cannot believe how incredibly rude that is!"

"Look," whimpered Carl, "I am so sorry, but I really have to go. Can I squeeze past you, please?"

"Fuck you, pervert!" shouted the man.

With a clenched fist, he delivered a powerful blow to the left side of Carl's face. With lightning speed, Carl soared across the hallway, his head colliding forcefully with the wall on the other side. The powerful blow hit him with such intensity, he saw stars. In a distressing moment, he experienced the embarrassing loss of control as his bowels emptied, resulting in an unfortunate spillage of diarrhea onto the hallway floor. As he lay there in his own excrement, on the dirty floor of the rooming house, a profound sense of humiliation washed over him.

A deep feeling of isolation and loneliness overcame him.

Chapter 16

"I'll have a large double, double coffee and a honey glazed donut to go please," said the short man wearing a lime green florescent coat. An orange construction helmet covered his head that seemed too tight for his skull. Carl smiled at him as he passed him his order. The man paid for it using the touchless feature of the credit card machine without checking the amount. "Thanks buddy," he said to Carl as he walked away.

Carl was feeling content with himself having a full-time job at Tim Hortons coffee shop. He had started after the unemployment assistance had run out six months ago. "With the extra money, I am now the proud resident of a one-bedroom apartment," he had said to Ray during the last session. "I could move out of that shit hole, and I can now have a shower every day! Just like the good ol' days."

"You certainly seem quite happy," said Ray.

"I constantly reflect on your advice about embracing the things I cannot change and making prudent decisions regarding what I can change. My life has become a series of unpredictable moments, as I live day to day. Every day, I search for something to appreciate and be grateful for. Initially, I found it challenging, but now I'm finding it hard to keep up with the abundance of good things occurring. Today was an example. As I was coming back from work, I stumbled upon a garage sale where I found a second-hand toaster selling for only $4. You have no idea how much I've longed for a slice of toast slathered with peanut butter and jam. It brings back warm memories of my children."

More than anything, he missed the sound of his children's laughter and the feel of their small hands in his. The label of "sexual offender" had made it easy for Andrea to convince the courts to prevent any contact.

Carl remembered the wide smile that broke out on Ray's face. Carl knew by Ray's reaction he had made significant progress through these weekly sessions. That was the main reason he stayed in the small town that had destroyed his life. Ray had been his lifeline, and he was not ready to let go of the thread that kept him stitched together.

Carl realized early on that he was barely hanging on, his grip slipping, his future uncertain. Years of operating had honed his clinical skills; he could methodically work through even the most challenging surgical complications. With colon surgery, five per cent experienced anastomotic leak with terrible pain and suffering for the patient. Some patients would die from septic complications, their bodies ravaged by infection. The reason for the post-operative leakage in some patients and not others remained a mystery, but every time it occurred, he blamed himself, his confidence shaken, questioning his surgical precision.

Carl meticulously reviewed the videos of the surgery following a serious complication. The sterile, clinical environment seemed to mock his search for a mistake; the surgery always looked flawless. A fleeting sense of calm might temporarily wash over him. But the return of the patient's sickness brought with it a wave of self-reproach, heavy as a shroud.

Following a bad surgical outcome, he often lay awake all night, tormented by pain and the worry of his future. The thought of the next morning filled him with dread. He knew the self-loathing would trigger waves of queasy nausea, agonizing stomach pains, and bouts of diarrhea. In the morning arriving at the hospital, the fluorescent lights hummed overhead as he trudged the sterile hallways passing the nurses and doctors, each step echoing the weight of a thousand judging eyes.

In their early days, Andrea offered supportive words and a consoling presence as he shared his feelings following a serious surgical complication, her touch gentle, her voice soft. For the past few years, though, he had silently borne the weight of his personal suffering, a heavy cloak of unspoken pain. If Andrea had known his thoughts, her predictable response would have been a sigh and an eye roll. "You are a weakling. That is why you can't sleep. Grow a pair of balls. If you can't handle the heat, get out of the kitchen. You should never have been a surgeon, anyway. Have you thought about that?"

The frustration of managing surgical complications was nothing compared to the profound grief and despair that had consumed him during the last six months. The intensity of Carl's self-loathing and humiliation was physical; a suffocating pressure in his chest. Ray declared he would overcome his challenges by focusing on small victories to make it through the day. He needed those small wins to keep his spirits up. It was like working through the surgical complications, the tension palpable as each decision felt critical. After a few days of rest and recovery, the surgical confidence would return, and Carl would be back to his old self, stronger than ever. Ray had cautioned him that this event would be a long, arduous process, requiring both time and resilience, but it was achievable.

When Carl tried to understand Sabrina's motivation, Ray had said, "You're a victim of circumstance," his voice heavy with the weight of unspoken understanding. "You may never know the reasons. It is like poring over the wreckage of a terrible car accident, examining every broken part and trying to piece it all together. You might find someone failed to signal a turn or check their blind spot, initiating a chain reaction of mistakes. In your case, the political climate has shown zero tolerance for sexual assault, with public outcry and swift action against perpetrators. The conviction felt preordained, a concession to the intense pressure from women's groups—the judge seemed to have no alternative. It's time to leave the past behind and concentrate on the task of reconstructing your life, focusing on each small victory along the way."

Carl realized he had been daydreaming when he felt a tap on his shoulder. It was Bob Jones, the owner and manager of the Tim Hortons restaurant. "Can I have a word?" he asked.

The store had quieted down after the morning rush and the two other cashiers could easily handle the orders. They walked to his office in the back of the store. "How are you finding things with the work here?" he asked. "You have been with us for the last 4 months."

Carl looked at Bob and smiled. "You have no idea how grateful I am for you giving me the position. It has made a world of difference for me."

Bob looked down at a piece of paper on his desk. He seemed uncomfortable, with his eyes moving back and forth from Carl to his desk. His right leg was bouncing in a nervous tic. Bob took a deep breath and blew it out slowly.

"What is it?" asked Carl.

Bob hesitated, as if not knowing where to start. "I received an email from an unhappy customer. In the email, she states she finds it offensive that you work here. She wanted to understand our rationale for hiring an individual who is on the sexual offender's list.

She is adamant about me firing you right away, concerned for the safety of the children from the nearby school who often visit this restaurant."

Carl remained silent at first, knowing this would be a tough conversation. "Look, Bob," Carl replied. "I appreciate everything you have done for me. You must do what you need to do and if that means firing me.... well, I understand. You gave me a chance when no one else would, and I will never forget that."

Bob looked at Carl shaking his head and said, "I am not going to fire you, Carl. Sure, you are down on your luck now, but you are turning things in your life around. I remember you coming into the hospital emergency room in the middle of the night two years ago when I had that perforated ulcer after my gastric bypass. That was the worst pain I had in my life. You took me to the operating room and fixed it. You didn't abandon me then, and I will not abandon you now. I just wanted you to know that you might hear about this complaint. I wanted you to understand my feelings about you working here."

Bob opened a bottle of water and took a large swallow before he continued. "We've both descended to rock bottom. For me, it was when I was bedridden from obesity with my eating addiction. You cured me of that with the gastric bypass. Look at me now." He stood up and turned around with his arms outstretched. "500 pounds, now down to 200 pounds. You turned my life around. Even when I became discouraged, you told me I could achieve my goals. That is all because you believed in me." Bob paused as if to collect his thoughts. "Carl, I believe in you, too. I wanted you to understand the reasons I am not going to fire you."

Carl stared at Bob, his eyes wide with disbelief. There really was something to the concept of searching for gratitude. "Gratitude is contagious, and as more people share it, its impact grows exponentially," Ray had told him more than once.

As Carl walked back to the front of the restaurant, he could hear the chatter of customers and the clinking of silverware. While he was engaged in conversation with Bob, a line had gradually formed. Carl took the person who was next in line. In just a matter of minutes, they served every person in the queue, resulting in no one being left waiting. Carl quickly glanced around the cozy coffee shop, taking in the sights and sounds. The sunlight streaming through the expansive windows that stretched from the floor to the ceiling brightly illuminated the room. The curved benches, which were a vibrant shade of red, provided a comfortable seating option for patrons who wanted to sit and engage in conversation. People could have private conversations by leaning across the small tables. Many individuals visit this place to enjoy a delightful ambiance that they can share with both friends and loved ones.

Sabrina, sitting in the far corner of the restaurant, away from the bustling crowd, had her eyes fixated on Carl, staring intently at him. In that moment, when their eyes locked, Carl experienced a sudden flutter in his chest, as if his heart had skipped a beat. Once again, he felt the familiar pain in his abdomen and an overwhelming sense of free-floating anxiety came rushing back to him.

Standing frozen with his mouth wide open, Carl witnessed her gradual rise and confident saunter towards him at the front counter. With her long blonde flowing hair resting on her shoulders and bouncing slightly as she walked, she maintained the same appearance as before. With a radiant glow, her bright blue eyes fixated directly on him. She moved across the floor towards him with such grace; it was as if she were effortlessly gliding on water. Her face wore a softness that Carl found difficult to interpret, as it showed no trace of emotion.

"We need to talk," was all she said.

Chapter 17

Carl opened his mouth to speak, but silence filled the air. No words escaped. Sabrina and he stood on opposite sides of the counter. The rows of mouth-watering donuts and muffins in a glass cabinet separated them from each other. The bustling sounds of patrons and servers seemed to fade away, leaving a serene silence that made the moment for Carl feel suspended in time.

Sabrina continued to stare at him, her eyes filled with regret, and said, "I never meant for any of this to happen to you. I have found a means to undo the damage that has been done. I'm going to walk back to the table in the corner where I was sitting before. It is of utmost importance that you listen attentively to my words. I want you to know that if, after 5 minutes, you decide you don't want to listen anymore, I will never approach you again."

Carl's mind cleared as she turned away and sauntered back to her table. He glanced at the CCTV camera that they placed strategically to be sure employees did not pocket any of the cash and to document the behavior of unruly patrons. Thoughts flew through his head. The terms of the parole included a condition he was not to contact Sabrina. *The video would show she approached me.* He looked and saw another CCTV camera pointed in the direction of the table where Sabrina sat. *This is too risky for me to consider. If I violate my conditions, they could put me in jail.*

As Carl stood there, Bob tapped him on the shoulder, causing him to jump. "Is everything OK? You look like you have seen a ghost."

Carl shook his head and said, "Can I talk with you back in the office?"

They walked through a door at the back and into the same office where they had their conversation several minutes earlier. "Bob, I need your advice. The woman that claimed I sexually assaulted her just approached me. She's sitting at the table in the corner over here!" Carl pointed to the image of Sabrina on the panel of video images in Bob's office. "She told me she has a way to undo the damage she has caused me." Carl glanced up at Bob with confusion in his eyes. "I'm grappling with indecision, unsure of the best path forward. As part of my parole conditions, I must refrain from any interaction with her."

Carl could see Bob looking at the video feed of the lone woman sitting at the table in the back corner of the coffee shop. No other patrons occupied any of the surrounding tables. She remained motionless but would sometimes glance over towards the counter where she had spoken to Carl. Scanning the other video feeds, there appeared to be no one else with her. A family of four occupied a table on the opposite side of the room. No one else was in the restaurant. The two servers behind the counter were engaged in discussion, but none of the videos recorded any sound.

"I have an idea," said Bob. "Why don't I talk with her and see what she wants? That way, you can make a more informed decision whether you want to discuss anything with her."

"You'd do that for me?" asked Carl.

Bob gave Carl a quizzical look. "After everything you have done for me? Are you kidding me?" Bob gave a wink to Carl. "Wait right here."

Carl watched on the video feed as Bob walked up to Sabrina and said something. Carl could see her motion Bob to sit down. He couldn't hear what they were saying, but it seemed to Carl that Sabrina was doing most of the talking. Every once in a while, Carl could see Bob nod his head. They seemed to talk for a while. Carl glanced at his watch. They had been talking for 20 minutes.

Bob returned to the office ten minutes later. He sat down. "Wow, what a story. Many of the details, she wouldn't tell me, and said she would only tell you. I think you should speak to her. I'll keep the video feeds in a separate file, so if we need to access it later, it will be easy to find. If I ever need to be a witness in the future to support you, I am happy to do this."

"What did she say?" asked Carl.

Bob shook his head and replied, "It's better she tells you

herself. It'll be okay. I'll watch everything from here. If you need me, just wave your hand and I'll be right there."

Carl thought for a moment. He trusted Bob. He did not trust Sabrina. Never had he understood the reasons she had filed the complaint. The closest he came to understanding her motives was that perhaps she mentioned what happened to someone she worked with who told it to Stephanie. Perhaps Stephanie put pressure on Sabrina to file a police report. Did Stephanie think it would advance her career? If that were the reason, Sabrina could have withdrawn the complaint before he got arrested. Perhaps a genuine apology, full of remorse, would have resolved the issue that troubled her.

Carl needed to find out. He got up from the chair in Bob's office and walked to where Sabrina sat. Sabrina looked up at him. There was a softness in her eyes, the same as when he was in the car with her on that fateful night. Without saying a word, he sat in the chair opposite her. He continued to stare into her eyes and said nothing.

She finally broke the silence when she said, "Carl, I am so sorry. I can only imagine the suffering and the pain I have caused you. I know how to make it right and I won't rest until I have made things better."

Sabrina looked down at the table. Her eyes became moist, and a tear ran down her cheek. She picked up the napkin and dabbed her eyes. "Let me start by saying I have not been totally honest with you. I work for a company in the Ukraine that has been involved with cyber attacks of hospitals. To prepare for an attack against your hospital, they asked me to report back to the company. By working in the OR, I could give them information about the computer operating systems, the security firewalls, and other digital information. Someone inside the hospital who knows what they are doing around computer systems can only access this information. The war in the Ukraine and Canada's sympathetic refugee program made for an ideal combination to position me and others like me in hospitals all across the provinces."

Sabrina paused, as if to collect her thoughts. "The cyber attack will begin on Thursday at 1 a.m. I need to stop it from happening. It could possibly bring down the health care system in Canada and too many people will suffer as a result. I am ashamed of what I have done, but I could not live with myself if more people suffer. I know I could possibly spend the rest of my life in jail if it comes out that I knowingly sent proprietary information to the Ukrainian criminals. But I swear to you, Carl, I did not know the extent of the criminal activities and the harm it would cause. I thought I would make a few hundred thousand in bitcoin at the end of all this and then slip back to Kiev to start a new life."

Carl looked at her incredulously, not knowing whether to believe her. Her shoulders slumped as if defeated. Her eyes glistened with tears and her face displayed genuine grief and guilt. She portrayed the signs of someone experiencing profound remorsefulness. He had misinterpreted her signals before, and that had been what had destroyed his life. He was not going to fall for that again.

Sabrina looked up at him. "You don't believe me, do you? I can see it all over your face. I don't blame you. There's more I need to tell you. Then I think you'll understand."

She wiped her eyes again with the napkin. "It is true I was in my last year of medical school in Kiev when the war broke out. It is also true I have a keen sense of reading people and I am rarely wrong. I was desperate to get out of the Ukraine. When the company approached me, they offered to help me get to Canada as a refugee and they said they would get me a job in a local hospital. They knew I had an undergraduate degree in computer science. Everyone thought the war would not last long and after Russia won, I could come back as a rich woman. They said all I needed to do was to provide them with some operational details of the hospital computer system. It became a lot more complicated when the IT department of the hospital beefed up their firewalls. The company needed a software developmental company inside of Canada to infiltrate the hospital perimeters and that is where they needed to take you out of the picture."

Carl, who had yet to say anything, was confused. He only had a rudimentary understanding of the hospital computer systems, just enough to navigate his way through the medical records and patient bookings. Not knowing anything about software, what she was saying made no sense. He shook his head as if to say what she described was simply unbelievable.

"You are mistaken about me," he said. "I know nothing about computer systems and software. You should have known that before you ruined my life. I don't believe anything you are saying." He could hear his voice rising, but felt powerless to stop it. "If you feel so badly, why don't you just go to the police and tell them? How does all this information help me? Even if I went to the hospital or the police and relayed what you have said to me, they would just laugh at my feeble attempt to clear my name. I've wasted my time talking with you." Carl was now yelling at Sabrina as he pointed his finger at her.

Carl got up to leave. He could feel his body shaking from his rising anger. A few customers at the counter turned towards him to see what all the commotion was about. *I need to control my emotions. This job is all I have right now.* Carl slowed down his pace as he walked away in an attempt to demonstrate to anyone who had witnessed his outburst and was watching him he was not a threat. He heard Sabrina shout at him as he strode away from her.

"You may know nothing about software, but your wife does," she said, raising her voice so he could hear her.

Carl approached the donut counter. "Do a Google search on her boyfriend, Jacob Friesner," she continued. "Only type in his real name, Vladamir Yursenko. She, too, is in grave danger."

Carl stopped in his tracks. He turned around and looked at the place where Sabrina had been sitting. Her seat was empty. Sabrina had vanished. All that remained was the scent of her Chloe perfume.

Chapter 18

"Carl," said Martin, "what brings you to see me? Is everything okay?"

Carl accepted Martin's handshake and smiled. "I mainly came for the view of the lake. It's worth the 3-hour bus ride just to see it. Look at the boats down there."

Martin turned and together they looked at the sailboats with their brightly coloured spinnakers on the expansive blue water of Lake Ontario from the 47th floor. "They are not supposed to fly spinnakers inside the harbour, so it must be an important race," continued Carl. He turned to face Martin. "The real reason I came to see you was to talk about Sabrina."

Carl relayed the story she had told him in the Tim Hortons restaurant. "Is there any hope of reversing the judgement against me?" asked Carl.

Martin leaned back in his leather chair and looked up at the ceiling. He seemed deep in thought. "The biggest problem is when somebody changes their story, the courts no longer find them reliable. They lied once, so they could do it again. You would need an independent source to collaborate with what she has told you. It sounds that might be difficult. Although she said the same thing to your manager, the courts would dismiss that as hearsay. I doubt she would confess to the courts she has been up to criminal activity just to clear your name. No one would believe her, anyway."

Carl felt crestfallen. He had just wasted a three-hour trip to Toronto.

"It would be expensive, possibly another $500,000, which you do not have. I don't see how I can help you."

"What should I do?"

"If I were you, I'd steer clear of Sabrina," he advised, a look of concern on his face. "Don't waste your time believing anything that comes out of her mouth. If her claims about an impending cyber attack are accurate, you may feel compelled to report it to the authorities or inform someone at the hospital. Be cautious, as they might accuse you of being involved out of spite or retaliation for the way they treated you, adding more fuel to the fire. If I were to offer you some advice, it would be to refrain from uttering a single word. If they ever question you about Sabrina, you could provide the same response as the courts and say, 'she had a history of lying, so it's likely she was doing it again'. It's highly unlikely that anything is going to happen anyway, so there's no need to worry."

"I looked up Vladimir Yursenko on the internet." Carl looked at Martin hopefully. "The US department of Justice has issued an arrest warrant for mail fraud and extortion. No matter how hard I searched, I couldn't uncover his whereabouts. I have no idea if he is the same person my wife is with, the one Sabrina claimed goes by the name of Jacob Friesner. Despite my efforts to contact Andrea, my voice mail messages failed to go through, and my emails bounced back. I need to warn her."

"Once more, it is highly advisable to refrain from getting involved in this matter. It is quite possible that she would not place much trust in your words, as she might perceive you as being resentful, angry, and intentionally trying to disrupt her fresh start. I think you are on your own in figuring this out. The courts made it clear that you should have no contact whatsoever with Sabrina. If you told anyone else about Sabrina, they could imprison you for violating your parole conditions. Andrea might report you to the police. Have you considered that?"

Martin glanced at his watch. "Sorry I cannot help you. I've got a 1 o'clock appointment, so you will have to excuse me. Good luck, Carl."

Carl got up and shook Martin's hand. "You gave me good advice. Thank you."

Martin guided Carl out of his office and to the elevator. The elevator doors opened with a soft ding. A television in the elevator blared the news. "The police are treating the death of the recent immigrant to Canada as suspicious and are conducting an investigation. If anyone has details about the recent activities of

Sabrina Hawryluk, the police are urging them to reach out."

A sudden jolt coursed through Carl's body as his heart skipped a beat. A sharp pain radiated from his chest, making it difficult for him to take a full breath. As soon as the elevator hit the ground floor, he swiftly punched the button for the 47th floor. It felt like the elevator was crawling at a snail's pace, as if time had slowed down. When the elevator doors opened, Carl rushed to the receptionist. "Please, I need to see Martin urgently!"

"Sorry, he's in a meeting," she replied calmly.

"Tell him Sabrina has been murdered. I saw her just yesterday. Believe me, he is going to want to know this." Carl could hear the panic in his voice.

The receptionist picked up the phone and pressed a button. She turned slightly away from Carl and whispered something into the phone. Within 10 seconds, Martin rushed out of the office and quietly escorted Carl into an empty conference room. Carl repeated what he heard on the news.

Martin sighed and looked out the window. "It's crucial for you to seek legal counsel given the circumstances. I am unable to continue representing you. Given your financial limitations, you must seek assistance from a legal aid organization. Ask Marg at the front to give you some numbers. I'm sorry, Carl."

Martin turned on his heels and stormed out of the room, the sound of his heavy footsteps echoing down the hallway. In the empty room, Carl sat there for a moment, the silence ringing in his ears as he pondered the events that had transpired. Martin showed no inclination to lend a hand. He knew that legal aid would only help if the police arrested him, or if they wanted to question him. With no help available, he had no choice but to navigate through this latest situation alone. Carl made his way out of the office and to the bus station to catch the 3-hour ride to his home.

With the late afternoon sun casting a warm glow, Carl arrived at the Tim Horton's coffee shop and politely knocked on the manager's door. "Bob," Carl said when he sat down. "They found Sabrina dead. They murdered her.

"I know," replied Bob. "The police were here. A customer recognized her and sent them here. I told them what happened at the restaurant. They want to talk to you."

"On no. I was to avoid all contact with her."

"I explained to them I spoke with her first and encouraged you to speak with her. The police were interested in the story she relayed to you about the impending cyber attack. I think they are mainly interested in what she told you. You have nothing to worry about."

Carl looked at Bob skeptically. "You think they are going to believe what someone on the sexual offender's list is going to tell them?"

"Listen," Bob said, "You have done nothing wrong. She approached you. You asked me to be involved, and I suggested you sit with her. I showed them the videos, and they agreed it seemed innocent enough."

Carl looked down at his feet. "Bob, I can't thank you enough for all the help you've provided me. I'm sorry for making you go through all this trouble."

Bob glanced around the room as if to be sure there was no one else around. "Oh, and one more thing, Carl... The police think she committed suicide. It was a devastating sight for her landlord to find her hanging by a rope in her living room, a tragic ending to her life."

Chapter 19

Jack Benner, the detective assigned to speak with Carl, had been waiting in his unmarked car when Carl arrived for work that afternoon and patiently sat at a table close to the front counter during the time he talked with Bob Jones. As Carl came out of Bob's office, the detective approached him and said, "Dr. Mackenzie. Could I have a word?" Following a discussion between Bob, Carl, and the detective, they decided Carl would be driven back to the restaurant after giving his statement at the precinct.

"There is no way she committed suicide," said Carl. They sat in a dimly lit interrogation room. The air hung heavy and still in the hot room, thick with the cloying scent of stale coffee and a hint of sweat. The detective he was speaking with wore a suit with a vibrant blue tie that caught his attention. With his calm demeanor, he exuded an air of control, effortlessly steering the conversation. While Carl recounted Sabrina's visit to the Tim Hortons restaurant, the detective's piercing blue eyes scrutinized Carl, as if trying to uncover any traces of dishonesty. In the small interrogation room at the local precinct, the flickering fluorescent lights cast long shadows across the faces of the two of them seated across from each other at the cold metal table.

"Why would you say that?" asked Jack.

"She seemed desperate to make things right. You need to

investigate the cyber attack and warn the hospital it is imminent." As Carl glanced up at the detective, he felt a knot forming in his stomach, a mix of nervousness and anticipation. Carl immediately knew it would not happen when he saw the skeptical expression on his face and the sneer lining his jaw. "Look, why would she tell me that if it wasn't true? She could go to jail if caught. I was there talking to her and I do not think she was lying."

The detective remained quiet. Carl shook his head. "At least give them the heads up. Something bad could come and you could leave it to them to decide whether they want to believe it. The guy to speak with is Fernando Rodriguez. He's in charge of IT at the hospital." Carl reached into his pocket and looked up the number and showed Jack. "Please, call him."

Jack punched the number into his phone and looked at Carl and said, "OK. I'll call him." Jack walked out of the room and out of earshot. Sabrina's image remained etched in Carl's mind, every detail vivid and unforgettable. *The concern written on her face was real as she described the potential harm a cyber attack could inflict on the patients. There is no way she could replicate that level of authenticity. They found her dead, her life taken away by someone who meticulously staged it to appear as a suicide. Then again, I have been proven wrong in my assessment of her before.* These thoughts swirled in his head when Jack returned.

"I told him what you said," replied Jack.

"And what did he say?" asked Carl.

Jack shook his head and sighed as though he had enough of this conversation. "He asked me what I thought. I told him I think it was all bullshit, but he said he would check it out."

Carl shook his head in exasperation. "What did he mean, check it out? Something bad is about to happen. Someone murdered Sabrina..." Carl looked down at his hands, controlling his emotions that threatened to derail the conversation. "... and I can tell you don't believe me. This is a bigger problem than just Sabrina, and I think you are missing the boat."

Jack's intense glare bore into Carl, his eyes filled with anger. "I'll drive you back now."

Bob was waiting for Carl as he arrived at the restaurant and ushered him into his office. "How did it go?" he asked.

Carl replied, "He didn't believe a word I told him."

Bob shook his head. "You know, I believed her too, when she told me she was concerned about the safety of the patients in the hospital." Bob looked at Carl with concern. "I don't think there is anything else you can do. You've done what you could and if something bad happens, it is on them. You warned them," he replied.

"Sabrina mentioned that the organization she worked for was interested in the hospital's operating system. Although I couldn't fully grasp the concept, she was discussing a process reminiscent of the two-step authorization used in online banking. They were seeking a reliable software developer from Canada to provide assistance. She insisted that my ex-wife played a role, but I find it hard to believe."

"The way Andrea treated you during your marital problems was far from the norm seen in healthy relationships. Forgive me for being bold, because I did not know her, but her drive for financial and personal success could easily have tipped her over the line to criminal activity."

Carl thought about that for a moment as he stared at a spot on the wall behind where Bob was sitting. He ran his hand through his hair as if it would clear his mind. "I don't think she would knowingly engage in criminal activity."

"Carl, based on your history, you tend to underestimate the lengths people will go to for financial gain. Dealing with the underbelly of society is a regular occurrence in my business, as I constantly encounter individuals who are out to manipulate and exploit me. In the restaurant business, where profit margins are tight, it feels like everyone is scrambling to maximize their share."

"I think there is something wrong with Andrea's mental

health. When I discussed it with my psychiatrist, he wouldn't comment on a diagnosis, only to say it would make little difference to me whether she was bipolar, borderline personality disorder or frankly psychotic. He encouraged me to accept that she wanted me out of her life and what was going on with her mental health no longer affected me."

Bob shook his head as if he didn't agree with Carl, but finally said, "If there is anything I can do to help, let me know."

Carl went to the front counter and served the customers, who patiently waited in line for their coffee and donuts. The afternoon and evening passed by quickly for Carl, as it was a busy welcome distraction. On his way home, Carl stopped for a slice of pepperoni with extra cheese pizza at the Pizza Pizza joint, the takeout around the corner from his apartment. He was about to take the first bite when news came on the TV that was blaring in one corner of the store. It was one a.m.

"Code Grey has been called at numerous hospitals across the region. This is the largest scale cyber attack to date." The middle-aged news reporter had a serious demeanor on his face, which revealed his underlying worry. "The cyber attack has left many of the computers with the name Ryuk in large white letters, leading experts to believe the attack originated in the Ukraine. Experts feel that the man known as 'the Russian' is responsible for the recent spate of cyber attacks across North America. His true identity is unknown."

An image of a long-haired, bearded man came on the screen. Under his video image was 'Alex Farrow- cyber security expert.' "They have installed ransomware," he said. "Cyber criminals are sneaky, lurking in the shadows until they find a weakness in a computer system's defenses to exploit. It entails identifying weaknesses within the operating system's code, which enables them to seamlessly implant their own code and bypass security or authentication procedures. They are requesting a staggering sum of $100 million to remove their ransomware. Patient information being exposed on the dark web is a genuine concern. They have done it before, and the knowledge from their successes in extorting money from other hospitals guides their actions."

Alex paused, his eyes fixated on the laptop that lay before him. "The Ryuk ransomware has taken over the entire hospital's digital systems, leaving no part untouched - from the patient's records to the X-ray department and even the internal phone system. Patients admitted to the hospital cannot undergo any tests, including CAT scans, bloodwork, or even emergency surgery. The cyber attack affects every area of the hospital."

"What advice do you have for the 20 hospitals?" asked the reporter.

John Hagen

"Pay them," was all he said.

Chapter 20

Carl basked in the warmth of the spring sunshine, feeling the gentle breeze caress his cheeks. It had been more than a year since he had last gone sailing, so the feeling of freedom that came with relying solely on the wind to propel the boat forward was incredibly invigorating. The boat, a magnificent 51-foot Hanse 508, named *ILEANA*, had state-of-the-art navigation and ocean-going equipment.

"She sails like a thoroughbred racehorse and seems to dance over the waves," Carl said to his friend Andy Appleby.

"She is very smooth indeed," Andy answered. "Feel the power of the jib pull us through the water. There is no feeling like it in the world, is there?"

Carl basked in the feeling of comfort as he felt the elegant sailing vessel gracefully cut through the blue waters. It was the first time since the events of the past year ruined his peaceful life that he felt a sense of inner peace. Two days ago, Andy called him and offered the opportunity to go sailing for the day. Without hesitation, he eagerly accepted.

"My boat, a 40-year-old C&C 35, went to the auction house and then the $38,000 check went into Andrea's bank account," explained Carl. "This feeling of being on the water, with the warm sun on my skin and the peacefulness of the surroundings, was exactly what I needed to soothe my soul. When are you taking her south?"

Andy went quiet. Carl glanced up at his friend and saw him take a deep sigh. His eyes raced around the horizon as if looking for something. His hands moved continuously, as if trying to find a comfortable position. "Sheryl left me. She kicked me out of the house. I've been living on the sailboat for the past 5 weeks."

Carl felt a pang of anxiety shoot through his body. "How is that possible? You guys were so together, the ideal Ken and Barbie team. The two of you told me you were sailing south, perhaps this fall or the next. I am deeply shocked. It must be tough for you."

"Well, the problems started when I lost my job two months ago. We started fighting. I really had lost interest in the job as an accountant. The boredom overwhelmed me. I knew I could not work in such a boring world of numbers. So, when she told me to get another job, I said no. I don't possess any other skills, except for sailing, and the boat is all I will get out of the separation."

Andy paused as he seemed to collect his thoughts. "When she went away on a business trip and came back early, she found me in bed with her sister. I tried to explain nothing happened. Her sister Sandy came over the evening before and we drank too much and passed out. I swear I didn't touch her, Carl. For Christ's sakes, we were both dressed. Sheryl hasn't talked to me since then."

Carl thought about his friend. They had been best friends at high school. At University, they were roommates in undergraduate for 4 years. Then Andy became an accountant and got a high-paying job in downtown Toronto, while Carl spent the next 10 years becoming a surgeon. They were the stars of the university sailing team at the RCYC, the yacht club the team belonged to during their undergraduate years. Carl would be at the helm, and Andy would be the crew of the racing dinghy, a 49er. They were both expert in their positions, with Carl making the tactical decisions and Andy managing the sail trim and spinnaker. Their frequent practice involved positioning themselves over the hull, with the cantilever technique, and utilizing their weight to gain maximum speed as the water flowed past them.

During a particular race, the winds were exceptionally gusty, causing challenging conditions for the participants. They were in first place as they rounded the windward mark. Andy prepared the spinnaker and launched it perfectly as they began the downwind leg, well ahead of the other competitors. Out of nowhere, a powerful gust of wind seized the spinnaker as the boat soared atop a massive swell and they became airborne. The boat flipped end over end as it nose-dived into the back of an enormous wave. Under the immense force, the hull split in half, and the vessel descended into the depths. Carl scanned the area in search of Andy when he surfaced, but unfortunately, he couldn't spot him anywhere.

He suspected Andy, still attached to the trapeze, was heading to the bottom of the lake with the sinking vessel. In a swift motion, Carl removed his life jacket and plunged deep into the depths, determined to reach Andy, who was in the midst of a desperate struggle to free himself from the trapeze. In a moment of desperation, when Carl felt like his lungs were about to burst, he mustered all his strength to release Andy's harness, enabling him to break free and make his way to the surface by jettisoning himself to the surface. Carl quickly followed.

Andy has made it his mission to do everything within his power to show his appreciation to Carl for the selfless act of saving his life. Despite Carl's recent misfortunes, he had extended a generous offer to let him stay at his house in Toronto. While Carl greatly appreciated the gesture, he wanted to focus on rebuilding his own life rather than becoming a burden to those around him. During all his troubles, he felt Andy was the one friend who had never abandoned him.

"I had no idea you were so unhappy with your work," said Carl. "It seemed clear to me you had a genuine passion for experiencing the best that city living offered. I thought you loved your job."

"Well, the unhappiness level has reached an all-time low.

Sheryl says I am having a middle age crisis. She doesn't want any part of my life now." Andy's eyes dropped to the instrument panel, as if he believed it held the key to unraveling the mystery of life and the solutions. Not finding anything, he cast a hopeful glance at the distant horizon, as if the answers he sought were teasingly close yet just beyond his grasp. Carl followed his gaze, his eyes scanning the horizon.

The gusty wind caused the sailboat to heel over, accelerating its speed to 9 knots. As the waves grew, Carl marveled at the smoothness of their motion and the way they cut through the water. The sailboat surged forward with determination, as if driven by a desire to showcase her full potential. The way she carried herself made Carl believe it was as if she had a mind and soul that were entirely her own. He felt a deep connection between himself, the elements, and the boat, as if they were all intertwined. It was a comforting feeling, being in control, as if all the fragments of his life were finally aligning.

"Wouldn't it be great to spend the rest of our lives out here on the water," said Carl. "Where else can we find this kind of comfort and happiness in this complex world?"

Andy smiled at his friend. "No such luck. It is better to absorb these scarce moments of inner peace and contentment. If we experienced this incredible feeling constantly, it would eventually lose its charm, and we would start searching for something new. Life is not so simple."

"I disagree," chimed Carl. "On the water, the conditions are constantly changing, as if nature itself is putting on a show just for us. It is an ongoing task to constantly adjust the sails for maximum efficiency. We need to be on the lookout for approaching vessels so as not to get split in two if they drove into us. In the past 5 minutes, we got hit by a gust of 22 knots and we heeled over even more. At that moment, I experienced a surge of excitement and adrenaline. I felt invincible, as if no problem was too big for us to overcome."

Andy became quiet again, as if digesting what Carl had said. Carl leaned back to rest on the cockpit coaming, so he could look up at the clouds. The puffy white fair-weather clouds indicated favorable winds and good sailing. He closed his eyes slightly and saw the clouds turn into images. He could see a poodle that seemed to turn into a tortoise. A Sheppard carried a staff and seemed to follow a flock of sheep. The cloud pattern appeared to turn into a map of the leeward islands of the Caribbean. He could see Antigua, St Lucia, Domenica and the Grenadines.

"What would you think about heading south with me in this sailboat?" asked Andy, shaking Carl from his reverie. "We could charter the boat for a week at a time. Four couples at $2500 per person would cover the expenses and give us enough to live on.

We'll be partners and split the profits 50/50."

Carl sat up and looked at Andy incredulously. "Andy, my name is on the sexual offenders' list for the next 10 years," he whispered, his voice filled with shame. "The harsh reality is this prevents me from crossing any country's border, leaving me with no options but to remain here until they lift it. If I tried to enter another country, they would boot me right back here. Another term of my suspended sentence was that I am not to leave the country until the end of my six-month suspended sentence." With sadness in his eyes, Carl shook his head.

Andy glanced up at Carl with a sparkle in his eyes. "So, you are interested," replied Andy excitedly. "The sentence will be up in a few months, and you will be free to leave then. As far as the sexual offenders' list is concerned, the Caribbean is full of much worse criminals than you. If they booted all the criminals out, there would be no one left on the islands. It might even give you an advantage having a criminal record." Andy chuckled at the irony.

"We would still have to travel through the United States, and they would definitely block me."

"I have thought of a plan," he said confidently, a mischievous glint in his eyes. "We would sail on a journey down the St. Lawrence Seaway and stay within our own borders. The goal would be to reach Halifax by boat and restock our provisions. The next stop would be Antigua, a mere 1800 nautical miles straight south. It would take us approximately 10 days to reach there. We would bypass the USA completely."

"Aren't you worried about hurricanes? This is hurricane season until the end of November."

"Leaving in early November is a possibility. When we reach the Caribbean, the hurricane season will have ended. A few of my ex-coworkers from the accounting company have already made reservations for a week. Four weeks in January and February have already been completely booked, showing high demand. Among my past accounting clients, I collaborated with a renowned marketing firm known for its innovative strategies and high-profile projects. The CEO and his family wasted no time in reserving their spot for the Christmas holidays, ensuring they would have a memorable vacation. He says he can help with the marketing. All I really need is a confirmation from you that you are in."

A medley of feelings surged within Carl, creating a whirlwind of emotions. The small town where he lived held little remnants of his former life. Sabrina's death completely eliminated any chance of him clearing his name. Despite having little hope of reclaiming his job as a surgeon, he had convinced himself that he would spend the rest of his life working as a server at the Tim Horton's restaurant. It was possible that Andy's plan could be the sole solution to escape from his wretched existence.

Conversely, he was gradually becoming more at ease with accepting whatever challenges presented to him in his new life following his conviction. Ray's weekly sessions played a crucial role in alleviating his crippling anxiety, ultimately enabling him to find joy even in the smallest moments of positivity. Agreeing to this venture would require him to leave his zone of comfort. Giving up his weekly session with Ray would be difficult. The thought of managing on his own, without Ray's guidance, filled him with uncertainty. His gaze shifted upwards to meet his friend's eyes, and a smile spread across his face.

"Count me in."

Chapter 21

"This is your last visit with me," said Carmine, Carl's parole officer. "I have to admit, you were the most compliant and co-operative parolee I have encountered in my 20 years as an officer."

Seated across from each other in the small office, Carl and Carmine exchanged glances over the polished surface of the wooden table. Carmine fixed his eyes on the laptop before him, his fingers dancing across the keyboard. With determination, he scrolled through the file, his fingers typing forcefully, determined to locate the information he was seeking. With a quick glance, he looked up at Carl.

"What are your plans, then?" he asked Carl.

Carl decided a long time ago to always be completely honest with Carmine. He had consistently shown respect towards him, despite being labeled a sexual offender. However, deciding to leave the country, potentially for good, may be seen as a blemish on his otherwise outstanding parole record, as per the parole rehabilitation philosophy. The success of a parole officer was measured by their effectiveness in facilitating a smooth transition back into society for convicted criminals, which included encouraging them to find meaningful employment and become active members of the community. Giving up the life Carl had built for himself could be interpreted as a setback.

Carl opted for the direct approach. "I plan to go on a sailing trip with my former roommate from university."

Carmine furrowed his eyebrows. "Where are you planning on going?"

"My friend Andy has a 51-foot sailboat, and he wants me to help him sail it to Antigua in the Caribbean. We will charter the boat for a week at a time. I will be the skipper, and Andy will manage the finances and scheduling."

Carmine stroked his goatee with his right hand as if thinking about what he should say. "Although the sexual offender's registry allows you to travel, some countries such as the US will bar you from entry. Have you thought about that? Perhaps you will sail all the way there and they will deport you back to Canada upon arrival."

As a bolt of anxiety rifled through his body, Carl glanced down at his hands, which were trembling uncontrollably. This was exactly what he was worried about. Linked to his passport, the sexual offenders' registry served as a permanent mark on his identity. Even though Antigua was not among the 100 countries that banned offenders from entering, he couldn't help but consider the possibility.

During his last session with Ray, they discussed his plans for sailing south. Although Ray did not explicitly express his approval, Carl could sense a subtle smile on his face, indicating his pleasure at Carl's bold decision to move forward in his life. This tacit approval from the person in his life he trusted the most confirmed he was making the right decision. Carl understood that life was filled with uncertainties, but he also he believed that without embracing risks, there could be no progress.

"I think that would likely be the least risk I would face." Carl met Carmine's glare as he continued. "We would sail at the tail end of hurricane season. The risk of nasty weather could result in the boat breaking, or in the worst case, sinking. Although we have all the necessary safety equipment, including emergency life raft, we could be at considerable personable risk doing this trip."

Carmine's glare intensified as he looked at Carl incredulously. "Have you lost your mind? You have made remarkable progress in securing a stable job, finding an apartment, and seamlessly integrating into the community. To abandon everything for the sake of rushing off to an impoverished country in pursuit of a better life is absurd. I must say, Carl," he sighed, "I am extremely disappointed."

The corners of Carl's mouth turned upward, forming a genuine smile as he locked eyes with Carmine. His intuition kicked in right away as he sensed what was going on. Carmine's focus had shifted away from his personal wellbeing and towards the daunting task of reporting the failure of reintegrating a convicted felon back into society. Carmine, like many others, prioritized his own interests above all else, even if it meant causing Carl to miss out on opportunities for personal growth.

"You need to understand what I have gone through, falling from the lofty position of a well-respected surgeon to a server at a Tim Horton's restaurant," explained Carl. "What happened to me was unfair and I think the recent cyber attack on the hospital confirms Sabrina set me up to cause a necessary distraction while she fed computer information to the criminals in her home country. Not dwelling on the miscarriage of justice, I wish to move on with my life. Although your 9 to 5 job might satisfy you, I need more than that. I need to have purpose and excitement in my life. This is the best chance that has come up and I am jumping in with or without your approval."

"Unfortunately, this leaves me with no alternative except to draft a detailed report that clearly communicates my strong disapproval of your actions. As part of my role, I aim to guide and support you in your journey towards becoming a respected functioning citizen, one that the system can take pride in. By choosing to take off, you are failing to fulfil your responsibilities and hindering your progress in your rehabilitation process. If you ever find yourself in the courts again, it is important to note that this report will not serve you well, and therefore, I strongly urge you to reconsider."

"You know they unfairly convicted me," replied Carl, trying to control his temper. "Yet you are still treating me like a criminal. It is clear to both of us I am innocent and have done nothing wrong. It's not honest to pretend that I need rehabilitation, when you of all people know what really happened."

Carmine slammed his hands on the table. His face went red and his nostrils flared. "It is not me who convicted you. I am a firm believer in the justice system or I wouldn't be here. You had a fair trial. They convicted you using the laws of the land.

"And how dare you suggest I have a boring existence as a parole officer?" Spittle sprayed from his lips, landing on the table in front of Carl. "At least I have a wife and children that respect and love me. You have nothing and are abandoning all hope of you ever becoming a father again by taking off on this fantasy trip. Carl, you are a failure and always will be. Now get the fuck out of here, you loser."

Carl's eyes narrowed as he shot a piercing glare at Carmine. The final parole visit turned out to be far from what he had anticipated. He knew it was unrealistic to expect Carmine's approval, but the intensity of his current fury was clearly abnormal. Carmine could have responded by acknowledging his disagreement and wishing him good luck as a way to part amicably. Bringing up his children was an inappropriate and unprofessional response, hitting below the belt. Carmine's pathological outburst served as further confirmation for Carl he was doing the right thing by heading south.

Without uttering a single sound, Carl stood up from the table and made his way towards the exit. A rush of liberation washed over him as he realized he was no longer bound by the system's demands, allowing him to forge his own path. Although his biggest regret was not being able to see his kids, he knew that someday, if he remained patient, the situation would change. He had the power to chart his own course, navigating whichever path that called to him.

As Carl walked into the Tim's Horton restaurant for his last shift, the familiar smell of freshly brewed coffee greeted him. The sun was high in the sky as it reached early afternoon. When he opened the door, a strange silence filled the restaurant, with no one to be seen behind the front counter. Glancing around the restaurant, Carl noticed the soft glow of candlelight on each table. Several tables away from the front, a couple engaged in conversation, their voices carrying softly through the air. Three high school students, seemingly skipping class, huddled around a table at the back, their attention completely absorbed by their cell phones. *The restaurant was mostly empty, but someone should have been at the front counter*, thought Carl.

In an instant, Carl's footsteps came to a halt, a sense of

unease washing over him. He cast his eyes around every corner of the store, but found no signs of anything suspicious. Slowly, he approached the front counter, his footsteps echoing in the quiet room. Suddenly, Bob, the two servers, and the three kitchen staff leapt to their feet from behind the counter, shouting in unison, "Surprise!"

Carl, caught off guard by the sudden startle, felt a wave of bewilderment wash over him as he involuntarily took a step back. With a quick, darting motion, his eyes surveyed each person in the group. They wore plastic inflatable rings around their midriff, giving them the appearance of swimmers ready to dive into a pool. As they closed in on Carl, the sound of their collective laughter and the feeling of their arms around him created a comforting cocoon. Some were saying, "We are going to miss you," with a hint of sadness in their voices. "Good luck on your travels," said the others.

Overwhelmed, tears rolled down Carl's cheeks, his emotions becoming too much to bear. He hadn't felt a sense of care from someone in what seemed like an eternity. A thought briefly crossed his mind, suggesting that he should remain in this place where he had a network of supportive and caring individuals. Perhaps the parole officer's assessment was accurate. He was leaving behind his safety net and embarking on a journey into uncharted territory. After a few minutes, they all went back to their work. As the kitchen workers rushed back into the kitchen, Carl took down each customer's coffee order, making sure not to miss a single detail.

Just as Carl's shift was coming to an end, Bob tapped him on the shoulder. "Can I have a word with you?" Carl nodded and followed Bob into his office.

"Carl, we are all going to miss you here," said Bob. "I want you to know you are welcome to come back if things don't work out for you down south. I looked up your boat on the internet and I booked a week in March for eight of us, my family and my sister's family, so you haven't seen the last of me. Keep me posted on how things are going."

Carl stood up and hugged Bob. "Thanks for everything, especially for having faith in me. When I saw what was waiting for me when I arrived today and the love that I felt from the group, I was having second thoughts about going. Now that I know you are coming to visit me in Antigua, I feel I have made the right decision about heading south. I'll take great care of you and your family for the best vacation of your life."

"Fair winds and following seas, my friend," whispered Bob to Carl as he left the restaurant for the last time.

Chapter 22

With the jib sail and a 3rd reef in the mainsail, the sailboat, *ILEANA* gracefully glided along at a speed of 10 knots, creating a fast journey towards the eastern end of Lake Ontario. The water was pitch black, and Carl could barely see anything as the autumn storm raged around him. Recognizing it would be a long night, he sent Andy below to catch some sleep. Blowing from the southwest, the wind caused the boat to sail at its fastest point, with the apparent wind hitting it from a perfect 90° angle. The boat's design was most suitable for sailing in heavy weather, which was crucial for their southbound journey. The first leg of their journey would require them to cross Lake Ontario, navigate through seven locks, and continue along the Gulf of St. Lawrence until they reached the vast expanse of the north Atlantic.

As they headed towards Kingston, Carl felt confident relying on the electronic charts and GPS to navigate the approaching shoals. The plan was to ride the coattails of the storm, using its powerful winds to sail eastward. The Iroquois lock, the first lock of the St. Lawrence Seaway, had scheduled their passage at 11 a.m. the next morning. If the winds were to cooperate, they could arrive well before the expected time, but it was crucial for them to remain alert and ensure they were well rested. In just 3 hours, Andy would take over from Carl, allowing him to get some well-deserved rest.

Carl could see the lights of Kingston as they flew past Amherst, then Wolfe Island, and into the narrow St. Lawrence Seaway. Carl glanced around but could not see the shoreline in the darkness, with the pelting rain obscuring his view. To be safe, he steered the boat to the middle of the channel, relying solely on the electronic charts to keep him from hitting the shore. The VHF radio came to life.

"Sailing Vessel Ileana, Ileana, Ileana, this is Cargo ship Ulysses on Channel 16," crackled the handheld VHF radio.

Carl turned on his headlight and grabbed the radio. "Ulysses, Ulysses, Ulysses, this is sailing vessel Ileana," Carl replied.

"Ileana, go to Channel 8," responded the voice on VHF radio.

Carl dialed into Channel 8. "This is Ileana on Channel 8," he said.

"Ileana, we are approaching you from the stern. Could you steer towards starboard by 200 meters so we can safely pass you to your port?"

"Will do," replied Carl. He spun his head and looked all around the stern, but there was nothing to be seen. Despite the ship coming closer, he could not make out any lights from it. While changing his course to starboard, he took a moment to glance at the electronic chart. From a distance of three miles, he could see the approaching vessel's icon on the electronic chart plotter. Carl, with a quick motion, clicked on the icon of the boat. The name Ulysses appeared. The AIS, also known as the automatic identification system, plotted the boat's speed at 20 knots while the CPA, the Closest Point of Approach, flashed, showing that the two vessels were on a collision course. In a matter of just 20 minutes, Ulysses swiftly surged past Carl, causing massive waves that violently shook the hull of *ILEANA*.

"Is everything OK?" asked Andy as he poked his head up from the companionway of the rocking boat.

"We just got overtaken by a cargo ship and the waves were huge," replied Carl. "Why don't you get back to sleep? You are not due to relieve me for another 1 ½ hours."

With a yawn escaping his lips, Andy made his way back to his bunk to rest. Over the next hour, the wind appeared to be less strong, causing the boat's speed to gradually decrease to a mere 6 knots. As soon as Carl started the engine, the boat's speed quickly increased to 8 knots. Once Carl's watch had ended, he felt exhausted and in need of a nap. Andy assumed control of the helm while Carl made his way to his bunk. It took him less than 30 seconds to fall asleep, and he remained fully clothed.

The alarm woke up Carl at 4 a.m. He felt like he had just lay his head on the pillow, yet it was time to get up to relieve Andy on the helm. Still dressed, he only had to pull on the foul weather gear and his life jacket to be ready for the watch. "I slept great," Carl said to Andy once he got on deck.

"We are about 15 miles west of the Iroquois lock," said Andy. "We can tie up on the wall once we arrive until they are ready for us. When I booked the 11 a.m. slot, they said if there was room for us, they could take us at 9 a.m. Now they are saying they may not take us until next week. This happens when government employees run the locks. With the biting winter winds fast approaching, we've got to get through the St. Lawrence Seaway quickly. The skies are clear and the wind has died down now the storm has blown through, creating a perfect weather window. This delay threatens to throw our schedule into complete disarray, potentially causing a cascade of negative consequences. I tried to explain the situation, but my words seemed to fall on deaf ears. The lock master in charge slammed the phone down on me."

"Shit," said Carl. "What's our strategy then?"

"We'll tie up on the wall and try to reason with them. If they refuse to let us through, we will barge our way in when they open the gate. I've done that before, but it could get ugly."

Carl laughed. "I'm used to ugly. Let's do this!"

The lock appeared on the horizon. The gates were open. Carl

placed the fenders along both sides of the boat. While Andy drove the boat hard to the lock before the gates closed. Two tankers had tied themselves to the wall of the lock. A space of about the size of *ILEANA* appeared between them. Andy aimed the boat for that space and Carl grabbed the attached rope with a boat hook. They fit perfectly with a foot to spare on either end.

A lock worker appeared at the top of the lock. His eyes were bulging and his face was red. "What the fuck are you doing? Don't you listen to your VHF radio. I said we are fully booked until next week and cannot take you."

Andy glared back at him. "We are here now," he yelled to the worker. "And we are not moving. You may as well accept that. We have plenty of room, so why don't you just start the process of lowering us along with the tankers to avoid any further delays?"

He stormed off, his footsteps echoing angrily on the concrete path, and likely went to call his supervisor. Within the next five minutes, the lock doors closed with a loud clang, and the water level in the lock slowly lowered, a gurgling sound accompanying the descent. Carl let out a sigh of relief, the tension visibly leaving his shoulders. When the doors opened at the bottom of the lock, Carl pushed off and they headed to the next lock, confident they would make it through the weather window before the winter winds arrived.

The Downfall

****

The rest of the experience of navigating through the locks of the St. Lawrence Seaway was flawless and with no further issues. As they sat in a cozy pub in Halifax, Andy and Carl took delight in the smooth and rich flavours of Alexander's Keith Brewery's famous pint. Six days of uninterrupted sailing had brought them from Montreal to their current location. It didn't take them long to get used to the 3-hour watch schedule, easily adapting to the new routine. It was in Quebec City where they filled up the fuel tanks with diesel. As soon as they reached the Gulf of St. Lawrence, the winds picked up and remained consistently blowing at a speed of 15-20 knots from the south-east until they successfully rounded Gaspe. Once they passed Gaspe, the winds changed direction, coming from the north, which made their journey to Halifax a pleasant and effortless sail.

"Our weather router, Chris Perkins, sent me an email this morning," said Andy, as he took a swig of the famous lager brewed in Nova Scotia. "He thinks we should be good to leave Halifax on the ebbing tide tomorrow morning."

"That sounds promising," replied Carl. He glanced up at the television screen in the pub's corner to see if there was a weather report. Not seeing one, he asked, "Did he say anything about hurricanes? Hurricane season is not officially over until November

30, and tomorrow is November 1."

"According to Chris," explained Andy, "A pocket of energy has developed and is currently south of Bermuda. However, he expressed doubt that it will develop into anything significant. Chris's impressive ability to forecast the trajectory of hurricanes gives me confidence that we could effectively navigate around it, even if it transforms into a hurricane. The reason it would be advantageous to leave tomorrow is because we will have favorable northwest winds that can safely carry us across the Gulf Stream. The scenario we absolutely want to avoid is when the wind is against the current. If the wind is from the east, this can cause the formation of massive standing waves that will have the potential to cause our boat to break in half."

"It will take us 2 days to reach the Gulf Stream as we head south. Will the northwest winds persist for the next few days?" asked Carl.

"They should stay with us for at least the next 5 days," replied Andy. "After that, the weather predictions are unreliable. With the Starlink dish on the stern of the boat, we can update the weather forecast every 12 hours."

Now, with the beer finished, they began their journey back to the sailboat, which was conveniently moored at the Royal Halifax Yacht Squadron. Recognizing the importance of getting sufficient rest before embarking on their 10-day voyage south, they opted to go to bed early.

While falling asleep, Carl reflected on the sheer luck that he had in being able to pursue his passion and do something he loved.

Chapter 23

A gentle, north-westerly wind, as forecasted, carried them safely across the formidable Gulf Stream. The sound of the Nespresso machine filled the air as Carl brewed a morning cup of coffee. Its delicious aroma instantly awakened his senses. Once they crossed the Gulf Stream, Carl immediately felt the drastic change in temperature. Carl had traded his winter attire for shorts and a T-shirt, feeling the warm temperature from the water.

ILEANA sailed smoothly on the warm winds, gliding at a comfortable 8.5 knots towards Antigua. With the autohelm engaged, the boat stayed on course without wavering. The chart plotter indicated 1200 nautical miles to Antigua. Carl found his way to the cockpit, where he positioned himself behind the starboard wheel, taking in the commanding view of the surroundings. Andy, feeling exhausted, decided to retreat to his bunk to catch up on some much-needed sleep.

The horizon, adorned with a scattering of fair-weather cumulus clouds, created an optimistic outlook for excellent sailing conditions in the upcoming days. The last report from Chis Perkins suggested the pocket of energy was moving towards the west. If it continued its current trajectory, Carl expected they would pass along the periphery of the depression in approximately two days. With the current weather, they expected reaching Antigua in approximately six days. They expected to come across a calm patch, devoid of any breeze, lasting up to twenty-four hours in a few days' time. Fortunately, they had fifteen jerry cans of extra diesel, ensuring they were prepared in case the doldrums lasted longer.

Savouring his coffee, Carl found himself in awe of the breathtaking sight before him - the endless sea, with no land in sight for 600 miles. As they sailed on a beam reach, the sensation of the gentle rocking merged with the sight of endless blue seas, made him feel intimately connected to nature. In the modern era of sailing, relying on electronic gear had become an integral part of the experience. With the latest advance of Starlink, they now could access the internet from any corner of the globe. It served as a safety feature for accurate weather forecasting and also offered the convenience of accessing Netflix for entertainment. So far, there had been no time for Netflix, as the day presented a series of small chores to keep them busy. Despite the constant wind, subtle shifts in its direction or strength necessitated constant adjustments to the sails for optimal performance and speed. The morning routine included a thorough check of the rigging, while also making sure to flush the water maker after filling the water tanks.

Carl discovered that by indulging in regular daytime naps, he could combat drowsiness during his 3-hour night shifts. On the ocean, he felt a sense of peace and contentment, with no one else to disturb his thoughts. This was a much-needed break from the burdens that had consumed him for the past year. As he glanced around the blue sea, he sighed deeply, taking in the vastness of the horizon in all directions. *This is what life is all about - experiencing moments of pure joy and contentment.*

Emerging from the companionway, Andy lifted his head and squinted against the bright sunlight. The furrowed brows and down-turned mouth gave away his deep concern. "I've just received a message from Chris Perkins via email. His instruction is for us to go even farther east. We are in the direct path of that intense pocket of energy, and it's rapidly approaching. If we set a course to 110°, we'll narrowly avoid it, but we'll still experience powerful winds of 30-35 knots. To prepare, he recommends putting in the 3rd reef tonight and partially furling the jib to about 25%. He says it could get rough after midnight."

"Are you worried?" asked Carl.

Andy glanced up at the sky and pointed. "Look at the mare's tails, the wisps of cirrus clouds high in the sky. They indicate that rain and inclement weather are on the way. But no, I'm not worried. This boat is solid. The winds on Lake Ontario were more powerful than the ones expected tonight."

"Since we'll both be on deck tonight, why don't you take a few hours to rest and then take over while I catch a quick nap? That way, we'll both be prepared for the strong winds when they come."

Andy nodded in agreement and headed below to his bunk. Carl adjusted the course from 170° to a course of 110°. The sails flapped in the wind, urging for a trim. After adjusting for the change in direction, the boat was now on a close haul. The sails were taut as they strained against the wind, desperate to outrun the approaching storm. The boat heeled over in the wind. To maximize the efficiency of the sail, Carl inserted the 2nd reef in the mainsail. While the speed of the boat stayed constant at 8.5 knots, the modifications allowed for less heeling and a more comfortable sail. *If the wind picks up anymore, I'll put in the 3rd reef.*

When Andy finally came on deck at 6 p.m. to relieve Carl, he had already accomplished the task of inserting the 3rd reef in the mainsail and had also furled the jib to 50%. Surrounded by the crashing waves, the boat soared through the water with a speed of 9 knots. With wind speeds reaching 25 knots and gusts as strong as 35 knots, it was quite blustery. Carl detached himself from the jack lines, which were securing him, and made his way to his bunk. As the sun had set, darkness enveloped the cabin. Carl fell into a deep sleep.

Startled out of his slumber by a blinding light that was immediately followed by a loud clap of thunder, Carl jolted awake. In a moment of confusion, Carl bolted up in bed, his head colliding with the cabin roof, until he finally comprehended where he was. Amid the pitch darkness, Carl felt the boat round up into the wind, causing it to bob wildly. Carl used his headlight to find his foul weather gear and life jacket before heading into the cockpit. Using his headlight, he looked around for Andy, but couldn't find him. "Andy!" he shouted over the howling wind. "Andy!" Panic seized him as he yelled.

The bright blue tether was hanging over the stern, still attached to the jacklines. Carl reached across the cockpit, grabbed the tether, and pulled. Andy was hanging off the stern of the boat, dragging in the water. Carl knew he would not be strong enough to pull him up by himself, but they had practiced man-overboard drills before they had left Toronto. Carl retrieved the blocks and pulley system that they had designed specifically for this. He attached one end to the boom, and the other end to the tether that held Andy. With the 8:1 mechanical advantage, he pulled Andy's lifeless body into the cockpit.

As Andy laid motionless in the cockpit, Carl's fingers gently pressed against the carotid artery, searching for a faint pulse. There was none. With a sense of urgency, Carl sprinted into the main salon, quickly retrieving the AED device and bringing it back to the cockpit. He swiftly removed Andy's jacket and shirt, then carefully positioned the electrode pads on his bare skin. Andy's heart was in a state of ventricular fibrillation, quivering chaotically within his chest. With a sudden discharge, the machine sent a jolt through the pads. Andy's body jerked off the floor, momentarily suspended a few inches in mid-air, before landing back in the cockpit. Carl's eyes quickly darted to the AED. The EKG revealed a normal sinus rhythm, indicating a healthy cardiac function. With a firm grip, Carl seized Andy's shoulders and vigorously shook him. Andy's face contorted as he forcefully expelled the salt water he had inadvertently swallowed, causing him to erupt into a fit of coughing.

Carl dragged Andy into the main salon and placed him on the cushioned couch. He was breathing better now, but still unconscious. Carl hooked up the AED to monitor the heat tracing. The oxygen probe showed his saturation was 92% and the pulse rate was 110. The blood pressure was 130/80. *Andy's vital signs were stable.* Carl's own pulse rate seemed to settle with that thought floating through his mind.

Carl turned on the switch to illuminate the main salon. Nothing happened. The boat remained in darkness. Using his headlight, he went to the electric panel, which usually had soft red LED lights to show which systems were drawing power from the batteries. No lights lit the panel. With a determined look, he pulled up the floorboards and inspected the batteries. The salon was hazy with smoke, making it difficult to see or breathe. The sight of the batteries, with their burst casings and charred marks, was evidence of a dangerous malfunction. They had transformed from their usual square shape into spherical forms, like mini planets. The smell of acrid smoke filled the air as it poured out from one battery. Carl quickly replaced the floorboard in an attempt to contain the smoke.

Carl checked on Andy, who was moving slightly now, but still not conscious. The vital signs were still stable, and the EKG looked regular. Carl climbed the steps to the companionway. The wind was shaking the mainsail mercilessly. The boat bounced around in the waves and from the shaking of the mainsail. Holding onto the cockpit table, he made his way to the helm. He punched the buttons on the instrument panel in front of the two steering wheels. They would not turn on. The auto pilot would not turn on either. Carl sighed. All the electronic equipment they depended on to get them to Antigua safely had been fried.

Carl went back into the main salon to check on Andy. "Andy!" he yelled. Carl grabbed his shoulders and shook him. Andy moaned and said something unintelligible. "I didn't catch that," Carl said. Andy lay on the cushioned couch. As Carl watched, he saw Andy attempting to sit up. "Keep laying down. You shouldn't get up," said Carl. Andy brushed him away with a dismissive gesture before sitting up. Leaning across the table, he rested his elbows and placed his head in his hand.

"I think lightning hit us," said Carl. "We have no electronics. I suggest we both go to bed and sort out in the morning what we should do. We are in irons now and the boat is in no danger." Andy's face was devoid of any emotion, wearing a blank expression. Carl, noticing that he couldn't walk properly, half carried him to his bunk, where he stripped off the rest of his wet clothing and carefully tucked him in. He watched Andy as he closed his eyes and emitted soft, rhythmic snores. Fifteen minutes later, with the assurance that Andy was safe, he made his way to his own bunk and settled in.

In just 2 minutes, Carl drifted off into a deep sleep.

Chapter 24

When Carl woke up, he could see the bright rays of sunlight streaming through his cabin window. As the boat bobbed up and down, Carl couldn't help but feel like he was floating on the water like a buoyant cork, with no forward motion. As he passed by Andy's bunk, he noticed he was still sleeping, breathing with a gentle snore. A check of his carotid artery revealed a bounding full pulse pumping at 80 beats per minute. *Normal. Now let's check the health of ILEANA...*

Upon entering the cockpit, he immediately felt the gentle caress on his cheeks of a mild 15-knot breeze blowing in from the east. Carl leaned forward to inspect the compasses in front of the steering wheels. They both seemed to work well. The boat was facing the east, directly into the wind, with the mainsail gently flapping as enormous waves from last night's storm rolled under the boat. Carl altered the boat's course and headed directly south, in the direction of Antigua. He removed the reefs in the mainsail and unfurled the jib. He felt the power of the sails pull the boat as she sliced through the water with a smooth motion, rolling gently with the swells that seemed to be spaced for a comfortable ride.

Carl anxiously pondered the uncertain duration of Andy's disability and whether it would leave a lasting impact. Having just seen the flash and heard the deafening crack of the lightning bolt,

Carl suspected it had knocked Andy from the deck into the water. The ventricular fibrillation was probably a result of being pulled unconscious through the water during the near drowning. Knowing that brain damage would result after four minutes without oxygen, Carl frantically calculated his chances of survival. The ticking clock was a stark reminder of the limited time he had. The timeline would be incredibly tight, leaving little room before permanent brain damage would result. Carl hoped the bewilderment clouding Andy's eyes would clear and the spasmodic movements in his shoulders ease, but it was too soon to know. The lack of battery power and internet access left Carl with a grim outlook on his ability to get Andy to safety, the silence amplifying his anxiety.

The autohelm relied on the batteries to function and now had no power. It would be impossible for him to hand steer the boat alone for the next 5 or 6 days it would take to get south. Thinking about how to manage this, he skillfully adjusted the sails, easing the tension on the mainsail sheet and tightening the jib sheet, ensuring the boat stayed on track without the need for constant steering. As Carl watched from the helm, he couldn't help but feel amazed at how the sailboat seemed to have a mind of her own, effortlessly guiding them towards their destination in Antigua. A sigh of relief escaped his lips, bringing a sense of calm to the tense situation. For the time being, he could temporarily step away from the helm.

Without an electronic chart, Carl had to rely on guesswork

to determine their location in the expansive ocean. Prior to GPS, sailors relied on the use of a sextant and tables to determine where they were. Nowadays, most boats lacked both. Suddenly, a thought flashed through his mind. Andy had mentioned the threat of lightning strikes and the potential for it to wreak havoc on the electrical system, leaving navigation futile. During their planning conversation for the trip, Andy had explained that the microwave would function as an effective Faraday box. "Placing devices inside a Faraday box ensured their safety from the powerful surge of a lightning strike," he had explained.

Carl was uncertain whether Andy had actually done this or if it was just empty words. They had a microwave on board, but it would only work if they connected it to shore power and had 110 volts. Since they hadn't used the microwave during the trip, Carl walked over to the galley and cautiously opened the microwave door. Inside, he found a handheld GPS, an Android cell phone, a portable lithium Jackery battery with 1500W output, and a small solar panel for recharging, neatly arranged. *One can never be too prepared,* he thought as a smile broke out on his face.

The handheld GPS sprang to life as Carl pushed the power button, its screen displaying a map of his surroundings. With bated breath, he watched as it powered up. The green screen flickered to life, revealing a menu that allowed him to track the sailboat's progress as it sailed south, represented by a small triangle icon. As he scrolled through the other options, he saw they were 1054 nautical miles north of Antigua, and confirmed they were on the correct course. They were travelling at 8.5 knots and would arrive in 5.16 days. Carl turned off the GPS to conserve power.

Carl checked the propane stove, and the flames refused to ignite. The propane stove had a safety feature that required it to be turned on using an electric switch, but the damage caused by the lightning strike rendered it useless. They had the option to cook on the separate portable barbeque on the stern railing of the boat, but right now, all he desired was the comforting warmth of a cup of coffee. Carl connected the Nespresso machine to the portable Jackery battery, and soon the machine hummed to life, filling the cabin with the delightful scent of freshly brewed coffee.

With his cup of coffee in hand, Carl went to check on Andy. Still laying flat on his back, he snored more vigorously, as if in a deep sleep. Carl shook him to see if he could wake him up. Although he grunted, Andy remained unconscious, refusing to come out of his slumbers. Carl went to the medical cabinet and carried the supplies to Andy's bunk. Using an orange rubber tourniquet, he inserted a 20-gage catheter into a large vein in his lower arm and hooked up in intravenous of .9% normal saline solution and ran the drip at 100 mL/hr. calibrated by counting the drops in a minute using his watch as a timer. *If Andy did not wake up in the next few hours, he would need to insert a Foley catheter to prevent overdistention of his bladder*. Carl needed some medical advice.

Tucked away beneath the starboard cabin bunk, he found the spare Starlink dish and modem. Carl carefully placed the dish on the deck with a clear view of the skies, ensuring nothing obstructed the view of the overhead satellites. With a simple connection to the Jackery battery, the modem came to life, emitting a faint glow. The dish moved, trying to lock onto a satellite in the vast expanse above. Using the spare Android device, he activated the Starlink, which Andy had paused until now. He instantly noticed the signal bars light up. Now that he had internet access, he could make a call to the hospital.

"Hello Jamie!" Carl said excitedly once he had connected to his former ICU colleague. "I'm 800 miles offshore in the north Atlantic. We got hit by lightning last night and I found my sailing partner dragging in the water, still attached to his tether. I pulled him on deck and found he did not have a pulse. The AED diagnosed ventricular fibrillation, and I activated a 200-joule shock. He bounced back into sinus rhythm. He seemed to wake up a bit last night, but this morning, he's unconscious. I've started an intravenous and have a few emergency drugs on board. I'm worried he might have cerebral edema. Do you have any advice for me?"

"Holy shit!" exclaimed Jamie. "You always seem to find yourself in the worst predicaments! I never believed all that sexual assault bullshit for one second, and neither did anyone else around here. Let me think for a second." Jaimie paused. "Do you have any dexamethasone and Lasix? If so, give him 8 mg of dexamethasone and 80 mg of Lasix. Repeat this in 8 hours, if no effect."

"Yep," replied Carl. "I have that stuff. I'll give it a go. Can I call you back if I need more advice?"

"For sure," said Jamie. "And Carl.... you should write a book about your story. Good luck!"

"Thanks Jamie," said Carl. He paused for a moment, thinking of what he should say. "And thanks for the vote of confidence in me."

Carl carefully placed the Starlink device back in its designated spot under the starboard bunk and unplugged the power source. He reached into the drug bag, feeling the cool plastic containers and the weight of the drugs in his hand. He pushed the medicine into Andy's veins using a port on the IV tubing, watching as it slowly flowed through the translucent tube. Carl anticipated the production of a large quantity of urine, so he carefully prepped Andy's penis with Betadine solution. With careful attention, he smoothly inserted a 16 F Foley catheter using a generous quantity of lubrication. Within seconds, the urine filled the catheter bag with a liter of clear urine. By 30 minutes, the Foley bag had drained 4 liters.

Within 2 hours, Andy was awake and talking.

Chapter 25

"We can probably fix everything within the next two weeks," said Peter, the chief mechanic at Electec Marine in St. Maarten. "Things are slow this early in the season, so you are in luck. When can we expect you?"

Carl replied. "We expect to go past the Simpsons Bay Causeway bridge at 8 a.m. tomorrow morning. Should we come directly to the dock at the Marina?"

"Yes, come right to us and tie up at the dock. We'll do an assessment and get a quote back to you within 24 hours. Then you can contact your insurance company with the quote."

"See you then," replied Carl.

Andy, standing in the cockpit, said, "I'm relieved we diverted to St. Maarten to Electec. Their facility for fixing boats is on a whole different scale compared to Antigua, with a vast space dedicated to repairs and maintenance."

Now that they had anchored the boat in Simpson's Bay, the sailboat swayed softly in the 10-knot wind, creating a soothing atmosphere. Although they had arrived earlier in the day, it was only a few minutes ago that they received customs clearance by email to enter the country. A wave of relief came over Carl when Andy got the email. *Maybe Andy's explanation about the Caribbean being full of criminals was the reason they let him in so easily, without having to answer troublesome questions about his past conviction.*

"What surprised me was how easy it was to get customs clearance online. You were right," Carl admitted. "They didn't seem to care about my status on the sexual offender's list." Carl shook his head in disbelief. "It would have been a terrible nightmare if they ousted us after all the trials and tribulations we faced to make it this far."

Andy smiled. "Imagine if you hadn't saved my sorry ass? How would you explain to the officials what happened to me?"

"They would have surely locked me away in a prison cell, branding me as a criminal for life. No one would have believed me if I told them what you had been through," said Carl. "Why do you think I was so desperate to keep you alive?" Carl laughed. "Saving your ass also saved mine!"

They lapsed into silence, each lost in their thoughts about the intense journey they had just experienced during the past five days at sea. An excruciating headache plagued Andy for a grueling three-day period before finally subsiding. Carl had to resort to intravenous morphine to ease Andy's intense headache, which was preventing him from getting any rest. Over those three days, Carl remained in the cockpit, tirelessly fine-tuning the sails to ensure the boat stayed on its intended path. On one particularly treacherous night, the massive waves forced him to hand steer through the rough waters. As the morning sun rose, he decided to hove to, effectively stopping the boat in its tracks and granting him a much-needed respite for a few hours of sleep. Exhaustion weighed heavily on him, making his eyelids droop and his body ache.

On day four following the storm, Andy's spirits lifted when the headache disappeared, and he eagerly offered to take over sailing the boat, allowing Carl to finally get uninterrupted sleep. After passing out for 6 hours, Carl finally relieved Andy, who was struggling to keep his eyes open. Andy's body craved rest after that first shift, and he slept deeply for a solid 12 hours, waking up feeling stronger and better than before. Seven days after the storm, they finally reached St. Maarten. From what Carl could gather, Andy seemed to have returned to his usual self.

"Let's go for a beer," suggested Andy.

The sound of clinking metal echoed as they fastened the spinnaker halyard, raising the dinghy effortlessly off the foredeck and dipping it into the calm water. Carl carefully maneuvered the dinghy to the stern, while Andy secured the powerful 9.9 hp Yamaha outboard engine. Once they had securely locked the sailboat, they climbed aboard the dinghy together. With no difficulty, the engine roared to life on the first pull, leading them to their destination at the Dinghy Dock Sailors Bar, where they happily settled down and enjoyed sipping on Heineken. Adapting to the sensation of walking on solid ground after carefully navigating each step on a constantly shifting boat would require some adjustment, but the experience of sitting on a stable platform was truly delightful.

"Don't you feel like a real sailor now that we made it here safely?" asked Carl. "We managed with just the bare basics in navigation equipment."

Andy looked at his friend and shook his head. "I have absolutely no recollection of what occurred after I got knocked off the boat. Until now, I didn't tell you this, but while I was having those terrible headaches, I wanted to give up. Overwhelmed by desperate thoughts, a sense of impending doom washed over me and I became convinced that our fate was sealed - we were going to die. I thought those were the worst days of my life until I remembered what you told me."

Carl looked at Andy quizzically and asked, "What did I tell you?"

"While you were going through your rough times, you told me what you kept repeating to your psychiatrist every time you saw him, 'This was the worst day of my life,' over and over again until he pointed out to you the obvious truth. 'This was the worst day of your life so far.' Your situation continually deteriorated until you eventually came to accept that life was about to get even worse. The moment you accepted your fate and actively looked for events that held significance and gratitude, you noticed a remarkable difference in the ease with which you navigate through life."

Andy paused. He glanced down at his hands and then directly into Carl's eyes. "Well, I did the same as you. While I suffered from the painful headache, I spent my hours looking for things to be grateful for. It turns out I didn't have to look too far. I am truly grateful for the way you took care of me, physically and emotionally."

Andy's eyes moistened. "It was as if the disaster of having lightning almost wipe us out was just another one of life's inconvenience for you to manage. I cannot think of a single person who would be in the same situation as you and not feel bitter and angry about the way things have unfolded for you in the past year."

"Ha," interjected Carl. "We made it here, both of us alive, didn't we? Our shared experience has had a profound impact on us, strengthening our resilience and empowering us to carry on. Think about it from my perspective, Andy, and the immense gratitude I felt towards you when I discovered that treasure trove hidden in the microwave while you were lying unconscious in your bed. We now could navigate. I could call a colleague for medical advice. It was even possible for me to brew a cup of coffee using the Nespresso. At the time of the crisis, I, too, didn't have to look too far to find things to be grateful for."

Andy stared at his friend. "Although going through difficult times is an expected experience in life, it is often only in hindsight that we realize things may not have been as dire as they appeared to be in the moment. Without a doubt, you exemplify that in the best possible way. Thinking about this daring adventure for us both to start anew, fully aware of the risks that might lead to our downfall, our faith in one another remains steadfast. I have a strong feeling that this is going to work out just fine. Both you and I know this to be true. I feel like I did as a teenager, full of confidence and invincible. I feel that way because of you."

Andy sat in silence; his eyes were moist with tears. He reached for his sleeve and gently wiped away the moisture, as if trying to regain composure. He lifted his glass of beer to his lips and gulped it down in a few big swigs.

As Carl listened to Andy, a wave of contentment washed over him, filling his heart with peace. It had been a while since he felt the warmth of appreciation and value from those around him. Positive feedback was a regular occurrence in the daily routine of working as a surgeon. Yet ironically, it was only since his professional downfall that he had a heightened sense of self worth. Carl attributed this to his habit of consciously finding things to be thankful for every day. Upon reflection, he realized that rising from the depths of despair and venturing into this new space had been a journey worth taking. He felt an unwavering confidence, as if he could conquer any challenge that came his way.

Carl made sure not to leave any beer in his glass before they headed back to their dinghy. They made their way back to the sailboat. As he drifted off to sleep, he held onto the belief that this moment could be the pinnacle of his new life, motivating him to continue in the relentless pursuit of gratitude to find happiness.

Chapter 26

Carl and Andy huddled around the desk in Jolly Harbour, Marina, Antigua, in the small office they had rented so they could look at the laptop together. They had lists and check marks on those tasks they had completed. "Food is more expensive here, but rum is cheaper," observed Carl.

Andy chuckled, "On balance, we'll be ahead, then. Everyone knows sailors are big drinkers and our $2500 fee per person is all-inclusive."

"So, if I understand correctly," Carl said, trying to clarify. "Our plan for tomorrow night involves you and I setting out to circumnavigate this stunning island of Antigua. We'll search for suitable locations to anchor the boat and to identify spots with excellent snorkelling opportunities. With over 360 beaches to choose from, Antigua offers a different beach for each day of the year, providing an abundance of options for us. The wind conditions and the direction of the swell will play a significant role in determining where we anchor on any particular night. Although it may require a few visits to gain the local knowledge of the best spots, I believe we are more than capable of rising to the challenge."

"For sure," replied Andy. "We have enough space in our fridges and freezers for 3 meals a day. We will probably only sail for 1-2 hours each day before we get to the next anchorage. The guests will no doubt want to get to the beaches and try the local cuisine at places like Sandals and other hotspots, so I doubt we'll have to cook for them every night."

"Our first clients are arriving in 2 weeks, so we will want to be prepared," said Carl. "That doesn't give us much time."

Andy's phone chirped. He glanced at the screen. "It's the electrician for the instrument panel," he said to Carl. Andy answered the call. "I'll put you on speaker so Carl can hear."

"The instrument panel on the port side refuses to power up," the electrician exclaimed, frustrated. "The starboard one hums along smoothly. I just spoke with the B&G manufacturer. He told me that the one they installed in St. Maarten is likely defective, indicating that a replacement may be necessary. Warranty protects all of it, so you don't need to worry. I'll take the defective one and get a replacement for you within the week."

Carl reminisced about St. Maarten, recalling the bustling commotion as locals worked tirelessly to mend the destruction caused by the lightning strike. They replaced all the exploded batteries with shiny, brand new lithium batteries. The engine's alternator and recharging systems underwent modifications. They completely overhauled the wiring for all the 12-volt functions, guaranteeing their smooth operation. Replacement was necessary for the electronic chart plotter, running lights, wind instruments, and a few lighting fixtures in the main salon.

The estimate of $75,000 quickly ballooned to a final cost of $110,000. Insurance covered most of the expenses, leaving only $10,000 to be paid. Andy was determined to switch to lithium batteries, enticed by their extended lifespan before needing to be recharged. The fried solar panels direly needed replacement, but once installed, the batteries would be fully recharged by the sun during the day, ensuring ample power throughout the night.

The result was an upgraded electric system that hummed with efficiency, ready to meet the demands of chartering and exceed the lofty expectations of the clients. After two weeks had passed, they finally prepared to leave from St. Maarten, embarking on an overnight sail towards Jolly Harbour in Antigua. Everything was working well, except that the instrument panel on the port side, in front of the wheel, when it suddenly went dark in the middle of the night. The sinking feeling in Carl's mind grew stronger as he wondered if this was just the beginning of another series of unfortunate events.

Carl, lost in his memories, abruptly redirected his focus when Andy interjected and carried on the discussion with the electrician. "We were planning on leaving tomorrow night for a week to check for good anchorages around Antigua for our first clients," said Andy.

The electrician went quiet for a moment, then said, "Why don't you meet me at the boat and I'll show you the issue. You will be capable of navigating using just the starboard panel, as it is working fine."

"I'll see you in 5 minutes," said Andy before he hung up.

"I'll stay here and finish up the list of food we will experiment with on our circumnavigation," said Carl. "We need to make sure we have enough choice to manage any client with specific dietary needs. Gluten-free, lactose-free, kosher meals, low fat and cholesterol-free, and anything else I can think of."

Andy left the office, the door closing softly, and Carl's attention shifted to the list of food items they needed to pick up tomorrow on the laptop screen. The crammed desk in the corner of the small office meant Carl sat with his back to the door. He heard the door open again. "That was fast," said Carl, not looking up.

"Hi Carl," said a woman's voice. Carl froze. *The voice was familiar. It couldn't be.....* Carl quickly turned around.

Andrea, his ex-wife, stood in the open doorway.

Carl's eyes widened as he stared at Andrea, his mouth hanging open in disbelief. His heart raced, and a wave of anxiety washed over him. His chest felt tight, and every breath was a struggle. The conditioned response he experienced upon seeing

Andrea, even after over 12 months with no contact with her, sent a jolt of surprise through him. Despite a year of intensive therapy with Ray and his newfound positive outlook on life, he still grappled with remnants of anxiety. It felt like he had transported himself back to square one, forced to relive the painful memories and undo all the progress he had fought so hard to achieve.

Motionless and silent, Andrea stood at the doorway. Carl could see her gaze fixed on him as she watched his surprised expression. Carl opened his mouth to speak, but his voice remained silent. As they locked eyes, time appeared to freeze, his focus solely on deciphering her unspoken cues and subtle gestures. Finally, after taking three slow deliberate breaths, Carl's anxiety settled enough for him to whisper, "Andrea, what are you doing here?"

Standing in front of Carl, Andrea's mouth slowly turned downward, and her eyes began to glisten with moisture. Her cheeks, stained with tears, streamed down like tiny rivers. As she reached into the pocket of her white shorts, her fingers trembled, grasping onto a tissue that would soon soak up with her tears. As her body transformed into a quivering mass, it was as if she could no longer hold back her tears and she sobbed uncontrollably, her whole body shaking.

"I'm in a heap of trouble," she said finally between sobs.

A rush of conflicting emotions washed over Carl. Seeing

someone suffer had always been difficult for him, but this time, he knew he couldn't offer her comfort. In the past, there had been an overwhelming amount of negativity that caused her to distance herself from him. All he could do was stand there, paralyzed, as he witnessed her unraveling before his eyes.

"Andrea, come have a seat," he said after a few minutes. "Let me get you some water."

Andrea wearily made her way to the chair in front of the desk, sinking into it with a deep sigh. Carl walked over to a compact fridge and grabbed a chilled bottle of Perrier sparkling water. With a gentle twist, he opened the cap, releasing a burst of fizzing soda, and handed it to her. She took a swig, which seemed to calm her. She looked up and said, "Carl...."

At that moment, Andy burst into the room. "It was a faulty connection. I can't believe it. There's nothing wrong with...." A gasp escaped Andy's lips as he stopped in his tracks, the sudden silence amplifying the sound of Carl's own heart. "Andrea? What..... what the fuck are you doing here?"

Upon seeing Andy, Andrea straightened her posture and composed herself. She delicately wiped away her tears with the tissue, trying to hide her emotions. Her composure transformed into a more professional demeanor, as if she was determined not to reveal any vulnerability in front of Andy. "It was from your website that I discovered where you were. I am staying at the Cocos Hotel right across the street from the Marina. I didn't know where else to go or who I should talk to... There was a direct flight here this afternoon. I'm rambling. Sorry...." As Andy and Carl fixated their gaze on her, she fell into silence. "Can we go somewhere to talk?" she asked after a moment.

"We can sit on the outside patio at Basilico," suggested Andy. "It's right outside." Andy pointed with his finger to the patio directly across a small walkway from the office. "It looks deserted this afternoon."

Shielded from the blazing sun by a brown canvas umbrella, the three of them settled down at a wooden table. A server appeared. Andy ordered a beer, Carl and Andrea asked for water. The boats caught Andrea's gaze moored at the docks; they swayed gently in the water's ripples, their sterns securely fastened to the dock with ropes. She pointed towards the boats and asked, "Which one of those is yours?"

"You see the boat with the gray hull with the name *ILEANA*?" replied Andy. "That's us."

Carl watched as Andrea opened her mouth to speak. She seemed tired. The belligerence she had exhibited during the last few months of their marriage had disappeared. It was almost as if she were a different person. "Huh," she replied and turned towards Carl and Andy sitting opposite her. Andrea shook her head as if to clear her thoughts. "I'm in trouble. Things did not go as I had hoped for."

Sitting motionless, she cast her gaze around the outdoor patio with uncertainty, as if grappling with the question of where to begin. Her eyes filled with fear, and Carl couldn't help but notice her pupils constricting in response. As Carl and Andy stayed silent, the weight of their unspoken words hung in the air, creating an uncomfortable stillness.

"What happened, Andrea," whispered Carl. "Why are you so scared?"

Andrea looked directly into Carl's eyes and said, "They want to kill me. I'll tell you what happened."

"Wait," said Carl. "Who is trying to kill you and why?"

"It's a long and complicated story, filled with twists and turns. Your suspicion of Jacob Freisner was well-founded; his shifty eyes and nervous demeanor eventually gave him away. It was too good to be true, a delicious lie whispered in the wind, promising something impossible. The signs were there, but I was too blind to see them at the time." Andrea paused as she glanced out at the boats in the marina.

"Go on," encouraged Carl. "Tell us what happened.

For the next 2 hours, Andrea's voice echoed across the table, interrupted solely by the sound of her taking occasional sips of water.

Chapter 27

"Do you believe what she told us?" asked Andy. Carl and Andy sat at the same table. Just a few moments ago, Andrea left and return to her hotel room. Despite the offer to walk her back in the dark, she declined the invitation. They had become so engrossed in her words they didn't even notice the sun had set an hour ago. No one else was on the outdoor patio. They had been talking for over two hours.

Carl disagreed, shaking his head, and added, "Throughout the years, Andrea has consistently been truthful. During our entire marriage, I have never once caught her in a lie. On occasions, she has withheld information. However, whenever she speaks, it is without a doubt the truth."

"This Vladimir Yursenko character actually exists?" asked Andy. "It sounds like science fiction to me. It's hard to believe he could live in Toronto under the radar of the police and get away with what Andrea has alleged."

"I have always believed Sabrina was murdered. Andrea has confirmed that tonight," replied Carl. "To ensure his tracks remain hidden, she said he chose to handle the dirty work himself rather than depending on someone else. I don't understand why it took her so long to see the signs of his true nature - a psychopath and murderer."

Andy seemed to think about that for a moment. "Carl, she was a mess when she walked away from you," his friend suggested. "Picture the gut-wrenching betrayal and disbelief she felt upon discovering your conviction for sexual assault; a violation of trust, now a legal reality. She likely admonished herself for not recognizing the signs earlier. Despite your years together, she almost convinced herself that the man before her wasn't the man she'd pledged her life to, a stranger in familiar clothing. She'd been the one to initiate the separation. Your conviction conveniently masked her guilt. From then on, a haze of emotion clouded her judgment, making it hard to see the subtle signs of someone's true nature. Sensing her vulnerability, Yursenko shrewdly used the money from the house sale to coerce her into building the software that facilitated the ransomware attack on the hospital's systems." A thick, suffocating air hung between them as they contemplated the evil implications of his actions, the silence punctuated only by their ragged breaths.

"Huh," said Carl. "That, along with her blinding drive to succeed at something, might explain her complete cooperation. It baffles me she could overlook the unsettling vibes and alarming red flags emitted by a psychopath for such a prolonged duration."

Andy was quiet while Carl reflected on Andrea's demeanor during their conversation. "Does she seem different to you?" Carl asked. "In the past, I would have expected her to go on a long rant about how unfair life is, magnifying the insignificant details and exaggerating minor problems. Instead, despite the terrifying experience she has endured, she displayed a remarkable level of composure and shifted her attention towards finding practical solutions to escape the chaos she found herself in. Somehow, to me, it seems out of character."

Andy shook his head. He appeared to reflect on their relationship and said, "I don't think I truly knew her well enough. The way she treated you was a shock, based on what you have described to me. This proves that you never truly know what secrets people keep within their own homes. Look at me and Sheryl, standing side by side, with smiles on our faces. We appeared to be the perfect couple, but beneath the surface, there were cracks in our relationship. When we're in public, we transformed ourselves, shedding our true identities and donning a mask of confidence."

"What do you make of what she said about the cyber security lead of the RCMP, Boris Arshenoff, being involved?" asked Carl.

"Well, she didn't exactly say that," replied Andy. "She said she went through Yursenko's phone and found he had called him on many occasions. There was the one occasion where Andrea followed Yursenko to a Russian bar, the Prava Vodka, and watched them have a drink together, but she has no idea what they talked about." Andy paused as if collecting his thoughts. "Although the partnership could explain how Yursenko could walk around in Toronto without fear of arrest for so long."

"It also explains why Andrea was reluctant to go to the police with what she knows," suggested Carl.

"Are you worried about your kids?" asked Andy.

Carl went silent while he thought. "Yes, very worried about them," he replied. "I know Andrea would do whatever is necessary to protect them. She says they are with her parents and they have taken every precaution to keep them safe, including housing them in a heavily guarded compound. She believed it was crucial not to disclose their location, even to me, until the threat subsided. Hearing her say that once this is over, I can see them whenever I wish, is something I never expected to hear coming from her lips. Now that she knows the about what happened, it gives me a sense of hope."

"Why should we even get dragged into this mess? The way she treated you was awful. Now she wants our help?"

"The weight of my children's well-being settles heavily on my shoulders; it's a constant worry. She is a kind and caring mom who nurtures the kids and provides everything they need. If for no other reason than that, I feel compelled to help her. The thought of my children growing up without their mother, robbed of her love and guidance, is a torment I could never bear."

"What are we going to do with this?" asked Andy as he held up the USB key.

"She never actually told us what's on the USB," replied Carl. "Just that it holds the key to the answers why Yursenko wants her dead. Should we have a look at it back in the office on the laptop?"

They left the patio after paying their drink bill and went back to their office and turned on the laptop. Andy plugged in the USB. "It is password protected," said Andy. "What do you think the password might be?"

Carl shrugged his shoulders then said, "She was always very secretive about her passwords, but let me try a few obvious ones."

Carl sat down in front of the laptop, the soft tapping of the keys filling the room as he typed in the names of the children. To gain access, he punched in various birthdates, searching for the correct combination. He tried their phone numbers and addresses of previous residences. Despite trying multiple approaches, none of them yielded any results. The USB key remained locked.

"We'll have to ask her for the password," suggested Andy.

Carl thought about it for a moment. "She doesn't want us to see what is on this," he said. "She said she wanted us to keep this safe until she needs it. For now, we'll keep it locked up in the safe on the boat where we keep our passports and money until she asks for it back."

"Hmmm," said Andy, "I guess there's nothing else for us to do for now. We'll have to wait until she contacts us again. She wasn't even clear how long she was staying in Antigua, or what she planned on doing next. Maybe someone is following her."

"I guess you're right. Let's go back to the boat. It's getting late."

They walked back to the boat, feeling the gentle sway beneath their feet, and made their way into the cabins. The sailboat boasted four spacious cabins, each equipped with its own private bathroom complete with toilets and showers. The boat provided these rooms for the guests' convenience. With no guests expected for the next 2 weeks, Andy decided to enjoy the comfort of the roomy forward cabin for a good night's sleep.

While Carl and the guests were out on a charter, the plan included Andy to stay ashore, sleeping on a pull-out couch in their small office. The sail locker at the bow had undergone a transformation, now serving as the captain's quarters, a cozy cabin complete with a compact stove and microwave. They tucked a small fridge and freezer under the single bunk. This was Carl's room, now cluttered with stacks of papers and an overflowing bookshelf.

The safe was in the captain's quarters, hidden under the bunk. Carl opened it and placed Andrea's USB onto the shelf and locked the door. Firmly mounted to a bulkhead, it was impenetrable, with its bolts securely fastened inside. Carl lay on the bed and placed his hands under his head. The anxiety he felt upon first seeing Andrea had long since dissipated. It was as if she had undergone a complete change, no longer finding any pleasure in pressing the buttons that unleashed his anxiety.

She seemed much more rational and willing to search for solutions rather than blame her shortcomings on others. It was almost like during the year apart, she had worked out her difficulties and could now cope better. The raw, unfiltered emotion pouring from her tonight–a torrent of joy, sorrow, anger–left him feeling unsettled; an icy dread spread through him. While he had managed to keep his volatile emotions in check this evening, he truly wished for her to remain unharmed and secure.

Tomorrow evening, Andy and Carl would leave the port in a mock circumnavigation as though they had guests. This was the long-awaited moment he had been anticipating ever since Andy extended that invitation on Lake Ontario six months ago. He was determined to make it a success, and not even the unexpected visit from Andrea could change that.

Chapter 28

Just outside of Jolly Harbour, Carl carefully dropped the anchor into the calm, protected estuary. The gentle breeze from the east kept the waves calm and small. As their week-long vacation began, the breathtaking sunset view from the boat's deck would greet the guests while they sipped margaritas. The extensive drink selection encouraged guests to pour their own beverages. Once the sun had disappeared below the horizon, they would gather around the table for dinner. Carl had thoughtfully prepared meals with a range of options, such as steak, fish, seafood, vegetarian, Kosher, and Gluten-free, accommodating everyone's dietary preferences. Andy and Carl's dinner tonight comprised a delectable lobster bisque, followed by succulent New York strip steak paired with garlic mashed potatoes and peas all the way from Guatemala. For dessert, they indulged in a slice of decadent red velvet cake topped with a scoop of creamy ice cream. Every night, the menu would offer a different selection of dishes.

The plan was to make the first meal and anchorage an unforgettable experience. Hopefully, the guests would exercise moderation and not consume an excessive amount of alcohol. They stored the drinks conveniently in the fridge and freezer in the cockpit. Following dinner, they expected some guests would gather in the main salon or around the cockpit table, engaging in conversation to foster new connections. Carl would always go into detail about the plans for the next day, making sure to include a thorough weather report. Tomorrow morning, they would set sail for Carlise Beach, a scenic destination just two hours away. Carl would offer a short historical overview of each destination, along with a list of possible activities to partake in upon arrival.

Every morning, Carl planned to rise before the sun, ensuring he was the first one awake to begin preparing breakfast. The breakfast spread included a variety of options, such as fresh pastries, cereal, fruits, and yoghurts. Carl would meticulously prepare each order, whether it was a fluffy omelette, perfectly scrambled eggs, or a stack of golden pancakes. Alongside the pancakes and eggs, the mouthwatering aroma of sizzling bacon and sausages would complete the menu. The Nespresso machine, filled with a variety of coffee capsules, would be readily accessible to satisfy anyone's caffeine cravings. In the cockpit fridge, there would always be a refreshing supply of orange juice. Andy, acting in the role of the shore coordinator, always ready to help, would bring supplies when they were running low, arriving in a 16-foot RIB powered by a 60 hp engine. The island was small enough that he could easily travel from one end to the other in less than an hour.

The package included snorkelling gear, but once they reached the beach, they had the option to pay for scuba diving, windsurfing, paddle boarding, and any other activities offered by the beach vendors. Salad and sandwiches were on the menu for lunch, offering a delightful combination of flavours and textures.

For 6 days straight, they would follow the same routine, waking up to the smell of freshly brewed coffee and the anticipation of another few hours at sea. One perfect anchorage after another until they arrive back at the marina for a new group of guests a week later. To prepare for the next group of guests arriving at 5 p.m. they had enlisted the help of locals to clean the boat and replenish their supplies of food and drinks. Their voyage would take them on a week-long journey completely around Antigua, allowing them to explore the most stunning anchorages in the Caribbean.

Andy and Carl, after a good night's sleep, pulled the anchor as the sun rose and they set sail for Carlisle beach, their first stop.

"What a beautiful morning," said Andy, sipping on his coffee.

"The wind is coming from the northeast, making this a perfect sail to Carlise Beach," replied Carl.

"What time are we to meet the taxi driver?" asked Andy.

Carl glanced at his cell phone and scrolled through some pages. "He's picking us up at 4 p.m. and driving us up to Shirley Heights. The van has enough room to comfortably seat 8 people, so I'm hoping there will be enough interest from the guests. For the 20-

minute ride to and from their destination, he is charging them $30 per person. Edward is providing his services free of charge today, with the expectation that we contact him every Sunday to arrange for the guests. I'll really hype up the experience so everyone will not want to miss it."

"When we get there, we'll lower the dinghy and see what the beach vendors are offering for kayaks, catamarans, and other water toys," replied Andy. "We can check out the snorkelling, and we'll speak with the divemaster about scuba lessons at the hotel."

Two hours had passed when they finally arrived in Carlisle Bay and set the anchor. The morning was absolutely stunning, with not a single cloud in sight and a brilliant blue sky stretching overhead. The beach, which was incredibly wide, appeared completely deserted except for a handful of umbrellas that were scattered across the sandy shoreline near the hotel. *This is what I have always dreamed about,* Carl thought as he glanced around.

When the clock finally reached 4 p.m., they found themselves positioned at the curb, patiently anticipating the arrival of Edward, the taxi driver, as he pulled up in his vehicle. As they embarked on their 20-minute drive, they passed by the exhilarating zipline nestled in the heart of the dense jungle. Carl couldn't help but make a mental note to bring it up when they had the guests on board. As they arrived at the summit of Shirley Heights, the joyful sounds of a steel band playing in the background greeted them. Excitement filled the atmosphere as tourists gathered, capturing the breathtaking view and stunning sunset with their cell phones. They couldn't wait to share these spectacular pictures with their friends back home, making them incredibly jealous of the experience.

Carl walked over to the stone wall and glanced at the sailboats in front of Galleon beach and English harbour. *This has got to be the most spectacular view in the world.* Carl spotted Andy talking to someone on the grass. He turned to him and shouted, "Andy, take a look at this view!"

He sensed Andy pull up beside him. Andy whispered, "Carl, we have a problem."

Turning around, Carl felt a wave of confusion hit him, causing his brows to furrow in bewilderment. Andy's eyes were rapidly moving, scanning his surroundings, and he had an overwhelming sense of fear emanating from within him. Carl quickly shifted his gaze towards the man who was standing alongside Andy. The familiarity struck him as he compared the picture he had seen on the internet to the individual standing before him, noticing the short blond hair and the pronounced jutting jawline. Carl felt as though the icy glare of the blue eyes penetrated deep into his soul due to its intense nature. The man was none other than Vladimir Yursenko. In a threatening manner, he revealed the gun that he had been pressing against Andy's back and swiftly concealed it afterwards.

"Let's wander over to there," said Yursenko. With a nod of his head, he gestured towards the stone building further back on the hill, away from the crowds. Yursenko, with the gun pressed firmly against Andy's back, led Carl and Andy towards the structure. After opening the wooden door, they walked in. In the center, there was a small table set up with a laptop placed on top. Yursenko closed the door firmly and secured it with a latch, ensuring that no one else could enter.

"Let's get right down to business," he said. "You have something that I want."

Carl and Andy stared at Yursenko without saying a word. He glared back at them. "Don't play dumb with me. Your bitch of an ex-wife gave you a USB. I want it. Here's what you are going to do. I'm going to stay here with Andy while you go back to your boat and get it for me." Yursenko looked at his watch. "You have exactly one hour, or your friend is dead."

"Where's Andrea! What have you done to her?" shouted Carl.

"You need only to do this one thing. Get me the USB," said Yursenko. His penetrating stare bore through Carl.

"I don't know what you are talking about," whispered Carl.

"You don't?" shouted Yursenko. "Well, maybe this will refresh your memory!"

Yursenko pulled out a large knife and, in a flash before Andy or Carl could react, he plunged it into Andy's left groin. Andy, as if in shock, stared at the knife that went in and out of the groin, and then he looked up at Yursenko. A scream escaped from his lips as he fell to the stone floor. Andy was softly moaning, pressing on the wound, not moving as he lay on the floor.

"I deliberately avoided the femoral artery and vein, but I won't miss them again unless you fail to bring me the USB," he shouted at Carl.

"Ok," quivered Carl, who felt a shock go through his body. "Let me check out Andy's wound before I go."

"Make it quick," replied Yursenko with a twisted grin on his face. "You have 58 minutes."

Carl squatted next to Andy. "Let me have a look," he said. Carl undid Andy's belt buckle and then carefully lowered his cargo shorts down to his knees. The knife had pierced the thigh, creating an open wound that appeared to be fairly superficial. However, the sight of fat bulging through the wound was quite alarming. Carl carefully examined the wound to assess its severity. The blood was coming from the edges of the wound rather than from a deeper area. The presence of a robust femoral and popliteal pulse led him to conclude that the arterial vessels were undamaged.

"I don't think there is any major damage, Andy," said Carl. "I'll bring my suture kit when I come back and I'll suture the wound. You are going to be alright."

Carl stood up and said to Yursenko, "I'll be back as soon as I can."

He opened the door and ran to the parking lot to find Edward sitting on the front bumper. "I need to get something from the boat. Could you drive me there and back?" asked Carl.

"Ok," said Edward, "But that was not part of the deal. You will need to pay me $100 up front."

Carl extended his arm, delving his hand into his pocket and retrieving his wallet. He reached into the depths of a deep fold and produced a fresh, new $100 bill, which he handed over to him. Afterward, he hopped into the waiting van and settled comfortably in the middle seat. As the sun had set, dusk quickly transformed into the darkness of night. Edward started the van and drove back to Carlise Beach.

During the time the taxi raced back to the sailboat, Carl found himself deep in thought, contemplating everything that had happened. Andrea secured her USB with a passcode, making it impossible to access. He wondered if Yursenko was aware of the secret passcode.

After locating the dinghy on the beach, Carl motored towards their sailboat that was anchored nearby, while Edward waited at the curb. Apart from another sailboat that had anchored further down the beach, the rest of the anchorage was devoid of any other boats. On the bumpy ride in the dinghy, he carefully formulated a plan, considering every likely outcome. By the time he climbed onto the boat, his mind was racing with a flurry of thoughts and strategies. He carefully packed the suture kit, antiseptic, instruments, and a few other things he would need into a backpack, ensuring he had everything he would need.

While planning their trip, Andy and Carl strategized about dealing with potential intruders. They considered the chilling sight of a weapon, the tension in the air, and the sounds of an attack. Though infrequent in the Caribbean, the possibility of a brutal pirate attack, with the sounds of clashing steel and screams echoing across the water, could easily ruin their entire business.

A suspicious-looking retired marine originally from Casper, Wyoming had befriended Carl and Andy. His weathered face was a roadmap of sea battles etched with deep lines and sun-baked skin. He suggested they buy some weapons, the cost of which made their jaws drop. A lively discussion over the price, filled with gestures and the occasional raised voice, ended with Carl and Andy settling on a few items. Carl carefully placed the heavy, oddly shaped items into the worn canvas bag slung over his shoulder.

He quickly leapt back into the dinghy, feeling the splash of the water on his skin. Edward had patiently waited for Carl, and when he hopped into the van, they left to go back to Shirley Heights. By the time Carl reached the stone building, he was slightly short of breath, his chest rising and falling rapidly. With a creak, he turned the doorknob and entered the room. The sudden flash of a bright light from Yursenko's headlamp temporarily blinded him, leaving him disoriented. Yursenko's voice echoed through the room as he shouted, "Give me the USB!"

Carl unzipped the backpack with a sense of anticipation, retrieving the USB stick and extending it to Yursenko. With his gaze fixed on Carl, he inserted the USB into the computer and then clicked on it. He shifted his eyes and allowed his gaze to wander over to the computer. "What the fuck...." He began. It was at this moment that Carl made his move. Taking out the taser gun he had brought from the boat, he quickly fired the electrodes directly into Yursenko's left neck. Yursenko's body convulsed uncontrollably, resembling a seizure, before collapsing on the floor. Using zip ties, he skillfully secured his hands behind his back and tightly bound his feet together. He used a third zip tie to securely fasten his hands to his feet.

Carl glanced down at Andy, his eyes almost popping out of his head in disbelief. "Are you OK?" Carl asked Andy. Andy simply nodded. "I'm going to sew you up here. It will take less than 10 minutes."

With steady hands, Carl grabbed the suture kit from the backpack and poured the antiseptic into a sterile bowl, ensuring everything was ready for the procedure. Placing the headlamp he retrieved from Yursenko on his forehead, he adjusted the strap to ensure it was snugly fitted and ready for use. With great care, he meticulously washed the wound to ensure its cleanliness. Andy winced in pain as he felt the antiseptic being applied. Carl withdrew 10 cc of Xylocaine and said, "This will sting for about 10 seconds." Andy winced once more, his face contorting in discomfort as the freezing sensation spread across the wound.

"I'm going to sew this up now. You shouldn't feel anything," said Carl as he began stitching. Carl used a 3-0 prolene stitch and within 5 minutes, the wound was closed. "Are you OK if we get out of here now?"

Andy nodded his head and stood up. "What are we going to do about Yursenko?" he asked.

Carl said, "He's coming with us. He is going to answer my questions." Carl removed the USB from the laptop and closed the lid. He placed both the laptop and USB in the backpack and handed it to Andy. "Can you take this?"

As Carl finished speaking, Yursenko moved slightly. Carl retrieved the taser and applied another jolt to the neck. Yursenko twitched as if having a seizure, then after 20 seconds, stopped moving. "I'll carry him," said Carl as he hoisted Yursenko on his back in a firefighter's carry. "You take the backpack."

As the tourists had all departed from Shirley Heights, Edward was the only one left in the deserted, dimly lit parking lot. "Our friend had too much to drink," said Carl. "We're taking him back to the boat."

Edward nonchalantly shrugged his shoulders before settling into the driver's seat. Once they were in the van, the sound of the engine roared to life as Edward expertly maneuvered down the winding road towards Carlisle Beach. When they were almost at the beach, Carl administered another taser jolt as Yursenko moved once more. Andy lent a hand, carrying him as they made their way towards the dinghy. Once at the sailboat, they dragged him up from the swim platform and placed him on the floor of the main salon, fixing his arms and legs to the table with more zip ties.

Andy and Carl went to their separate bunks and fell asleep.

Chapter 29

"Help me! Help me!" shouted the voice coming from the main salon. Carl glanced at his watch. The clock read 5 a.m. as the world remained cloaked in darkness. He groggily crawled out of bed, slipping on a worn T-shirt, cargo shorts, and well-worn sandals. A gust of salty sea air hit him when he crawled out of the hatch leading to the deck. As he entered the main companionway, he flipped on the light, temporarily blinding Yursenko. In the tense silence, they locked eyes, each waiting for the other to break the stillness with words.

Yursenko's face twisted into a sardonic smile, as if a realization hit him - it was Carl who had abducted him. "You have no idea who you are fucking with," he whispered.

Carl smiled back at him. Yursenko was sitting on his knees, the hands and feet still bound together with zip ties and secured to the salon table behind him. "That may be so," replied Carl, "But I am about to find out."

Andy appeared in the doorway of his cabin and glared at Yursenko. "Let's get a move on then, Carl," he said.

Carl flipped on the running lights and the mast light, illuminating the boat in a soft, warm glow. Then he started the engine, and the low rumble reverberated through the air. With a firm hand, he engaged the gears and set the engine in motion. As Andy raised the anchor using the windlass, the boat slowly crept forward. Carl swiftly turned the wheel, causing the boat to make a sharp 90° turn. It now set sail towards the south, leaving the shore behind. It was pitch black, and Carl couldn't see his own hand in front of his face. They motored until they reached the open ocean, 5 miles away from the shore. The boat swayed gently as the east swell rolled beneath it.

"Let's get him," said Carl, as he put the boat in neutral. Andy and Carl went into the main salon and cut the zip ties that attached Yursenko to the table and carried him onto the deck. They sat him at the table in the cockpit, one on each side of him, so he couldn't move.

"We are going to ask you some questions, and you are going to answer them," said Carl. "We'll start with some easy ones."

Yursenko kept a stony expression on his face and said nothing, staring directly ahead.

"How did you find us?" asked Carl. "If you followed Andrea, how did you know we would be in Carlisle Bay? How did you know we would go to Shirley Heights?"

Yursenko said nothing and continued to stare ahead. Carl nudged him with his elbow and asked again. This time Yursenko responded with, "You have no idea how much trouble you are in.

I'm not answering your questions."

"Have it your way," replied Carl.

Andy and Carl pulled Yursenko onto the cockpit floor and tied a line around his ankles. Using the same block and tackle apparatus Carl had used to rescue Andy after the lightning strike, the two of them pulled Yursenko in the air, attached only by his feet upside down. His arms were still bound by the zip ties, and although he was struggling, he could not move very far.

"Before we dunk you in the water upside down, I'll ask again. How did you find us?"

"Fuck you," was the response.

Carl and Andy released the rope and Yursenko plunged into the water headfirst. The force of the fall sent a powerful wave of saltwater splashing into the cockpit, soaking everything in its wake.

Andy glanced at his watch. "We'll let him soak for 30 seconds, and then we'll pull him back."

After a mere half minute, Andy and Carl hoisted him out of the water, their hands dripping with cold droplets. Yursenko gasped for air and forcefully expelled water from his throat, coughing uncontrollably. As he emerged fully out of the water and hung upside down, fear became visible on Yursenko's face. Carl and Andy stared at him while they waited for a response. Once Yursenko finished coughing, he whispered defiantly, "Fuck you!"

Carl and Andy released him into the water again. "We'll see how he does with 45 seconds," said Andy as he glanced at his watch.

After the seconds slowly passed, they pulled him out. This time the coughing was more violent and when they shone the light on him, his face was a purple colour. Each cough had him jerking on the line tied to his legs. Carl and Andy were having difficulty hanging onto the rope from all the spasmodic movement from Yursenko's coughing. After 5 minutes of coughing, his colour improved. Carl asked again. "Are you ready to answer my questions?"

Yursenko shook his head and tried to say something, but no words would come out. "Let's dunk him again," said Andy. Fear spread across Yursenko's face. He began shaking violently. Carl and Andy started lowering him into the water when he yelled in his raspy voice. "No! I'll answer whatever you want!"

Carl and Andy carefully guided him onto the boat, helping him settle onto the soft cushions of the cockpit bench. Andy's fingers swiftly retrieved his cell phone from his pocket, ready to film the sight before him. Yursenko, shivering from the cold and trembling with fear, appeared oblivious to his surroundings. His defeated posture was evident as his eyes remained fixed on the cockpit table; his shoulders slouched. Carl opened the fridge and reached for a bottle of Perrier water. As he opened it to him, he could feel the condensation on the cold glass, making it slightly slippery in his grasp. Yursenko's hands shook as he gulped down the water. Some of it escaped and dribbled down his chin. Yursenko cleared his throat, then belched loudly.

"So, how did you find us?" asked Carl.

"Finding you was easy using your AIS on the boat, and your Google timeline," he said with a trembling voice.

"Thank you," said Carl, satisfied with the answer. "Why did you kill Sabrina?"

Yursenko looked at Carl with pleading in his eyes, as it was obvious he did not want to answer it. He glanced at the block and pulley apparatus still dangling from the sailboat's boom. He sighed deeply and then answered. "She threatened to expose the entire operation. We had invested too much by then and we couldn't take a chance."

"Next question," said Carl. "Where's Andrea?"

"I don't know." Carl looked at him suspiciously. He could see panic in Yursenko's eyes. "That's the truth," he said, his voice filled with conviction. "We started out together. I convinced her to embark on a software product venture, explaining the purpose aimed at revolutionizing the healthcare industry. What it actually did for us was to provide us with unrestricted access to the electronic medical records of the 20 hospitals. In her mind, she saw herself developing a product that would be a lifeline for patients in need. When she discovered that her software development caused the cyber attack, she panicked."

"What is on the USB?" asked Carl.

Yursenko went quiet for a moment and his shaking intensified. He looked up at Carl. "The $100 million in bitcoin the hospitals paid us went missing. It happened around the same time that Andrea disappeared. I think it was Andrea who took the bitcoin. She is the one who would know how to do that. The information to get the bitcoin back could be on the USB."

"The USB is password protected. How would you gain access?" asked Carl.

"That was what the laptop was for," replied Yursenko. "The team of cyber security experts was ready to log onto my laptop and crack the code. That is why you are in such big trouble. Even if you kill me, they will come after you. Your lives are meaningless to them."

While lost in thought, Carl absentmindedly rubbed his chin with his hand. Not having shaved in a few days, he could feel the prickly stubble on his jaw. "Who is this team of cyber security experts?" asked Carl.

A hush fell over Yursenko, his silence speaking volumes. His body trembled with even greater intensity than when they initially pulled him from the water. Genuine fear was evident in his eyes as he vigorously shook his head. "I've already told you too much. My life is over now. I do not even know for sure myself who they are, except they will try to track me down and silence me. I promised I could get the bitcoin back. That was the only thing that prevented them from killing me. This was my last chance. Once they realize I didn't succeed, well...." Yursenko halted his sentence abruptly, his head drooping in disappointment. Carl could feel his defeat weighing heavily on his shoulders.

It was clear to Carl, as he glanced at Yursenko, that further discussion would be futile. Carl fixed his gaze on a man who appeared utterly defeated, with his head hanging low. Carl knew the feeling all too well, as the same woman who had outsmarted him had outsmarted Yursenko. Despite knowing it was irrational, Carl couldn't help but feel a pang of sympathy for him. Continuing the conversation with him would reveal no further useful information.

Carl started the engine, and the roar of the motor filled the air. He set course for Carlisle Beach. When they finally arrived 45 minutes later, the rising sun bathed the landscape in a soft glow. The trade winds, gentle and warm, whispered through the palm trees from the east. Andy dropped the heavy anchor, causing a loud splash that echoed across the calm sea.

"We are going to drop you off on the beach," said Carl. "If anything should happen to Andy, Andrea or me, the video of your confessions will be all over social media and every police force in the world. It would be in your best interest to keep us alive."

They loaded Yursenko into the dinghy and before they reached the beach, they removed the remaining zip ties to free his arms and legs. They lifted him over the rubber tubing and threw him in the water close to the shore. The water was 3 feet deep. While heading back to the sailboat, they spotted him trudging wearily towards the beach. He slumped down on the sand, his head drooping in despair, capturing their gaze.

Back at the boat, they turned off the AIS and their Google timeline. "What should we do with Yursenko's laptop?" asked Andy.

"I suspect they could track us if we keep it," replied carl. "Let's heave it overboard."

Andy retrieved the laptop from Carl's backpack and brought it to the deck of the sailboat. He threw it into the water with a splash. Andy held up the USB. "What should we do with this?"

Andy handed the USB to Carl. Carl's arm tensed and he launched it into the water with a sudden, forceful throw. Andy's jaw dropped as he gazed at Carl, unable to believe what he was seeing. Carl shrugged his shoulders and said, "Let's get the hell out of here."

Chapter 30

Carl and Andy anchored the boat at Galleon Beach in English Harbour, surrounded by crystal-clear turquoise waters. After an hour-long journey from Carlisle Beach, they finally arrived. At least 20 anchored boats dotted the remote beach, adding a sense of serenity to the surroundings. Despite briefly considering returning to Jolly Harbour, they were hesitant, fearing that those searching for the missing bitcoin could easily track them down. Preferring to hide in plain sight, they cleverly disguised the *ILEANA* name by covering it with the letters *CARLA*. Turning off their AIS, they became more elusive and difficult to locate.

"What is our next step?" asked Andy.

"I am certain that Andrea will contact us soon," replied Carl. "I'll leave my cell phone on. We need to find out more about Yursenko and those that work with him. Whether or not we like it, we are deeply involved now."

"What do you think will become of Yursenko?" asked Andy.

"He's a survivor. He will retreat into the shadows, lurking in the hidden corners of the world, patiently awaiting his next chance. I do not think we will ever hear his voice again. We need to worry about those others he mentioned who seem determined to go to any lengths to claim their portion of the $100 million."

Andy glanced at Carl with a puzzled look on his face. "You seem remarkably confident in a good outcome. Carl, it's time to face the truth. We have no idea what the hell we are doing. We are flying by the seat of our pants against unknown forces that would crush us like stepping on a bug." Andy's voice had risen as panic seemed to take over. Concern etched his face, deepening the lines around his eyes and mouth.

To calm his friend, Carl gently placed his hand on his shoulder. With a soft voice, he said, "One thing I learned as a surgeon is that no matter how skilled or self-assured you are, the result of a surgery is always uncertain. While a flawless operation could lead to someone's demise, a poorly executed one could, surprisingly, yield an excellent outcome. As a surgeon, both scenarios would make me doubt my skills and expertise. Many times, I contemplated giving up on surgery, but then I came to the realization that there are external forces at play determining the course of events that are not within my control. Right now, we find ourselves in that very situation. What sets us apart is that we have the advantage over the others."

"That's crazy thinking. Have you lost your mind? What possible advantage do we have over these ruthless criminals?"

"We have something they want from us."

Andy looked at Carl with a confused expression on his face.

"Are you talking about the USB you launched into the ocean? If so, there goes our leverage! The only thing that is keeping us alive is at the bottom of the ocean floor."

"Let me show you something," said Carl.

Carl led Andy into the main salon and they sat at the table. As Carl opened his laptop, he heard the faint hum of the fan starting up. On the desktop, Carl's cursor hovered over the icon labelled 'Andrea' before he clicked on it. A series of computer code appeared on the screen, flickering with each line. As Carl's fingers danced across the keyboard, an icon depicting a lock materialized on the screen. By clicking on this icon, a prompt appeared, asking for a password. As he entered the correct password, the screen flickered and a new account window appeared, ready to be explored. With a few flicks of his finger, he navigated through the files on this account until he settled on one to click. The label 'account balance' positioned itself directly across from the jaw-dropping figure of $100 million.

Andy watched speechlessly as Carl worked. When Carl looked up at Andy, he could see his mouth agape with an incredulous look on his face. Andy stuttered out the words, "What the.... What have you done? How did you.... How did you do that?"

"When I came back to the boat to retrieve the USB to give to Yursenko, I uploaded the contents onto my laptop, then wiped the

USB clean. That's why Yursenko was so surprised when he opened the USB and found it had no files. I knew it would be my opportunity to immobilize him with our taser, during that moment of confusion."

"I don't know what to say. What happens now?"

"I still have the contact cell phone number for the Minister of Health, Aaron Cohen, from when I was the president of the surgical society. I spoke to him this morning before you got up. He surprised me by answering, and it surprised me even more when he listened to me. I sent him this file." Carl tapped on the icon labelled 'Andrea' to demonstrate the point. "This morning, his team of cyber security from the ministry will handle the task of transferring the bitcoin account back into the government coffers. To ensure protection from future cyber attacks, they have heightened the firewalls surrounding the medical records."

Andy sat back and exhaled. He looked at Carl with concern. "By doing that, haven't you just jeopardized our leverage and sealed our fate? If those who terrified Yursenko are solely focused on retrieving the bitcoin, don't you believe they will resort to violence and vengeance against us?"

"First of all, they won't believe we would do something like that. The lure of financial gain blinds criminals to the fact that not everyone shares their same motivations. They might suspect that we are secretly hoarding the bitcoin for our own purposes, and we could potentially use it as leverage if necessary. As a surgeon, when I was faced with events that were seemingly out of my control, I found that doing the unexpected often had the best results. The sound of beeping monitors in the operating room would allow me to think clearly as I made a split-second decision to deviate from the standard procedure. The tension in the room was palpable, but ultimately, it was the right move."

Carl and Andy stopped talking as if to assimilate everything they had shared. Andy kept shaking his head as he got up and made a Nespresso. "Do you want one?" he asked. Carl nodded his head in affirmation.

Carl was sipping the coffee when his phone chirped. He answered it. The caller ID said it was Andrea. "Carl, I'm in a heap of trouble," she whispered. "Even more than before. Can you help?"

Carl listened intently to what she had to say, remaining silent for a moment. After a few minutes, he said, "Let me talk to Andy. And we'll meet you there. Give us 15 minutes." Carl hung up the phone.

Carl glanced at Andy and said, "She wants us to meet her at the Antigua Yacht club, on the patio. I think it is a trap, though."

Andy looked at Carl in confusion. "Why would you say that?" he asked.

"She asked me to text her when we got there. She gave me her phone number and the last number should be an 8 and she said 7. She knows I have her number, so why would she give me the wrong one? I think it was a warning."

"What are we going to do, then?" asked Andy.

"We'll have the element of surprise," replied Carl. Carl relayed his plan to Andy. With everything in place, they pushed the dinghy into the water and set off. In just 10 minutes, they arrived at Nelson's Dockyard and locked the dinghy there. They walked the 300 meters to the Antigua Yacht Club, greeted by the sound of clinking glasses and laughter. As they passed by the super yachts, the sound of the water lapping against the hulls filled the air.

They painted the large pillars in front of the Antigua Yacht Club in bright yellow and blue colors, which perfectly matched the table and chairs on the patio. A colourful array of bright yellow and blue umbrellas shielded the hot Antiguan sun, providing shade for the patrons. Carl and Andy sat at an empty table. He texted Andrea. "We are on the patio."

A minute later, his phone pinged. "I'll be there in a minute." It was from Andrea.

Carl and Andy sat in tense silence as three burly Antiguan men slowly made their way towards the table. All of them had smooth, bald scalps. The oils they had applied to their scalp made their black skin glisten. Their eyes hid behind the large Ray-Ban Wayfarer sunglasses. The expressions on their faces revealed nothing. Their arms and chests strained against the white t-shirts, almost as if they were about to burst through the fabric. The one in front beckoned, "Come with us."

Carl glanced at Andy. He remained seated. "Where's Andrea?"

The largest of the men flicked his head towards the super yachts tied up at the yacht club. "She's over there. Come with us and you can see her for yourself."

Standing up, Carl and Andy hurriedly followed the large men, their footsteps echoing on the empty wooden patio. They strolled along the docks and encountered a massive 95-meter Lurssen super yacht named *WHISPER*, its name proudly displayed on the stern. In the sunlight, the hull of the boat gleamed and reflected a dazzling shine. Luxurious furnishings and the soft glow of the chandeliers greeted Carl and Andy as they were escorted into the main salon of the boat. Positioned in the heart of the room, Andrea sat quietly on a sleek, white leather sofa. It had been 2 days since they last saw her, and she was still dressed in the same clothes.

The zip ties cut into her skin, restricting her movement and causing discomfort. In a cruel act, they had forcefully placed a gag in her mouth, rendering her unable to speak.

Chapter 31

Carl stopped in his tracks, his eyes widened and his mouth agape. "Untie her," he shouted. "Andrea, are you OK?"

As Andrea's eyes scanned the room, they captured the fear that gripped her. With a fleeting glance, she communicated her remorse to Carl, her eyes filled with apology. It was a surprising and unfamiliar feeling coming from the person who had previously brought him so much pain. A thought flew past Carl at that moment. *There is something noticeably changed about Andrea; I cannot pin down what it is.*

A bodyguard's sudden grasp met Carl on his approach to Andrea, propelling him forcefully onto a comfortable leather sofa. "Sit!" he commanded, his voice firm and authoritative. Carl glanced at Andy, watching the intimidating stature of the 3 massive men, their muscled arms crossed as if daring Andy to resist. Andy resignedly sat down beside him.

"Welcome to paradise," boomed a loud voice from across the room. A large man in his mid fifties appeared, the voice echoing off the marble walls. Carl turned his head. The man had a large potbelly and a thick neck with rolls of fat hanging from his jaw. The many years of excessive indulgences were evident as he waddled to the center of the room. Carl suddenly knew this was the man known as the Russian, the one behind the cyber attacks.

"We have a slight problem. I am hoping you can help us with it," he said, smiling. He had a thick Russian accent. "My good man Yursenko promised me he would take care of it, but he somehow disappeared." The man stopped mid-step. "You wouldn't possibly know what happened to him, would you?" Carl's blank, expressionless stare seemed to prompt him to say, "Yes, of course not."

Motionless, Carl became engrossed in the unfolding theatrics before him, the sounds and sights captivating his attention. Surprisingly, Carl felt a sense of calm instead of the expected anxiety from the past as he faced yet another impossible situation. The feeling of control filled him with confidence and determination. It was clear to him that this man was the instigator of the cyber attack, and the one to blame for Carl's downfall. Confronting the demon that had orchestrated all this sent a surge of satisfaction through him. Carl's calmness and rational mind remained unchanged, reminiscent of his earlier experiences in surgery when confronted with seemingly insurmountable challenges.

In that moment, he found solace in the assurance that his self-confidence had returned after so long. Despite this being his first encounter with this self-indulgent pig, Carl was confident that he would be the one in control today.

"You want your money back?" asked Carl.

The man glanced at Carl and clapped his hands. His rolls of fat on his face twisted in a sarcastic smile. "Very good! You seem to be with the program now."

"It must cost a lot to have a boat like this," said Carl, his hand sweeping around the expansive. "Is that why you need the $100 million?"

"The boat is such a small part of my fortune, but yes, this extravagance is something you will never experience in your lifetime."

"What is the cost of, say, Sabrina's life, when you live in such luxury?"

"Her life was worth about $100,000 to Yursenko." The man sighed, "But it was all for nought, until I get the money back. Andrea was kind enough to tell me it was on the USB she entrusted to you." His face darkened and his pupils constricted. The contortion highlighted the fat in his jowls, making his eyes seem to retract into his skull and become even smaller. "Now hand it over!"

Carl glared at him and then said, "There is something I want to show you." Carl pointed to the large screen on the wall at the front of the salon. "Can you turn that on?"

The Russian gestured towards the nearest bodyguard, motioning for him to activate the screen. His eyes sparkled with amusement, their twinkle reflecting the mischievous expression on his face. With a click, the screen blinked on and displayed a vibrant image. Carl pulled out his cellphone, his fingers tapping on the screen as he found the screen mirroring icon. Within seconds, the television screen flickered to life, displaying a live newscast. Holding a microphone, a blonde woman commanded the attention of the room. She stood outside of the Ontario legislature.

"In a surprising twist of events," she said. "The $100 million that the Ministry of Health had paid to the cyber criminals found its way back into the ministry's coffers. Here is Aaron Cohen, the Minister of Health, to explain."

The camera focused on the minister. "This morning," said the minister, "I received an email that contained detailed instructions on how to retrieve the $100 million in bitcoin. We had paid this amount to safeguard the medical records of the patients at 20 of our hospitals."

He cleared his throat, then continued. "The payment was essential to ensure that the criminals did not release them onto the dark web. Since then, we have taken measures to fortify the security systems in all the hospitals across the province, minimizing the chances of another cyber attack. I promptly forwarded this to our cyber security team at the ministry, seeking their expertise. They were successful in the retrieval of all the money. We are still ironing out the specifics of what took place, and I will provide you with updates as soon as more information becomes available."

The reporter asked, "Who was responsible...." Carl stopped the newscast and flipped the screen to Facebook. The Russian's face instantly appeared on the screen. Carl watched his face turn crimson as the camera recorded his reaction and sent it live to 100 million viewers worldwide.

"Facebook has the live recording of the past 15 minutes," said Carl in a calm voice. "Your face and those of your bodyguards are now broadcasting to everyone who tuned into the news about the cyber attack. It will probably reach over 500 million viewers by tonight. Your reign of terror is over."

As he stormed out of the room, the Russian's body convulsed with intense shaking, a clear manifestation of his rage. In a final act of anger, he pointed directly at Carl, his finger trembling, and shouted to the three bodyguards, "Eliminate them!"

As Carl stood up, he could see the looks of confusion slowly taking over the faces of the three bodyguards. Glancing at each other, they silently communicated their hope that one of them would have the answer on whether to proceed with carrying out the Russian's order to kill them. Their hands were fidgeting, unsure of where to rest or how to occupy themselves. Carl felt a wave of unease as the bodyguard closest to him narrowed his eyes and took a threatening step forward. The others stood by, their faces filled with a sense of helplessness as they watched the turn of events. Carl held his hand up in a commanding stop gesture, signalling for the bodyguard to halt.

"Look," said Carl. "Anything you do now, the camera fixed to the pocket of my shirt will record for the world to see. I would be very careful about your choices. You are getting recorded now. My advice would be to go home and look for another job. This boat is to be seized for a police investigation into the murder of Sabrina Hawryluk and an investigation into the cyber attack in Ontario. The Canadian RCMP constables are flying in now to cooperate with the Royal Police Force of Antigua and Barbuda."

The two bodyguards closest to the door glanced at each other before racing out the exit. Carl could hear the pounding of their feet as they ran down the docks. The last bodyguard, upon seeing his friends desert him, spun around and joined them, running away on the docks. Carl watched with a satisfying grin on his face as the room filled with silence. He walked over to Andrea. He opened a drawer in the cabinet against the far wall and found a sharp knife. The knife easily sliced through the zip ties and released her. Andrea tore the gag from her mouth and burst into tears. She leaped up and hugged Carl, sobbing with convulsions.

"Thank you, thank you. I knew I could count on you to do

the right thing," said Andrea.

Chapter 32

Saying that the publicity they gained from dismantling a cyber criminal network was good for their chartering business would be an understatement. The social media platforms depicted them as valiant warriors, fearlessly defending the virtual realm from malicious cyber stalkers. Despite receiving invitations to come to talk shows across the US and Canada, they chose not to accept. Building their business was their top priority, and Carl and Andy dedicated countless hours to its success. The phone never seemed to stop ringing, so they finally hired a secretary to manage the calls. Carl and Andy sat at the bar of Basilico's outdoor patio, enjoying the refreshing taste of their ice-cold beers.

"We have enough clients to fill six boats every week for the next 6 months," complained Andy. "What are we going to do?"

"Do you think that had anything to do with the Minister of Health petitioning the courts to get me removed from the sexual offender's list?" asked Carl, trying to make light of his improved status.

"Ha, ha," replied. "Your status was a curiosity factor and generated a lot of interest from some of the less scrupulous women clients. Now you are off the list..... well. But don't worry, the office has filtered out those that could be potential problems. No way we are going through a repeat episode of connecting you to unsavoury women."

Carl smiled as he thought about that for a moment, then changed the subject. "Look over there," he said, pointing to the sleek catamarans from Dreamboat Vacations. "It has been a month since they last took on any clients. I asked Tommy, the dockmaster, for some information, and he informed me that the company had gone bankrupt. We could probably get them at a steal since the bank has repossessed them. All of them are under five years old, and Tommy says they are in excellent condition."

Andy suddenly became animated. Carl could see him scrolling through some numbers in his head. "If we could get them at a good price, say $300,000 each, we could still make 15% profit per week. With seven boats, including *ILEANA*, we would get $20,000 per week profit. With year-round business, we would be multi millionaires within a few years!"

The following day, they met with the bank manager, who had a tired look in his eyes from a long day of repossessions. Finally, removing the six boats from the liability dockets thrilled the bank manager. Successfully selling them to Andy and Carl gave him one less thing to worry about. The surveys uncovered some deficiencies, causing the set price to drop even further. The previous captains of the catamarans, who were still without work, gladly accepted the invitation to join Andy and Carl's company. Within a month, Andy and Carl's company fully booked every charter, with reservations extending all the way until April of the following year.

They moved into a larger office and rented a nearby storage facility to house their supply of linens, towels and other items. Both Carl and Andy would remain on shore to coordinate a smooth vacation for the clients by running supplies to the boats when they became low and troubleshooting problems as they occurred. The skippers of the boats would also be the cooks and sports activity coordinators.

In the office on a Tuesday, Carl could hear phones ringing and keyboards clacking. So far, they had chartered all seven of their boats, and everything was running smoothly with no hiccups. The door to the office swung open, and the bright light from the windows flooded the room, illuminating the desk. Andrea walked into the room with Carl Junior and Simone, their laughter filling the air.

"Daddy. Daddy" they both shouted in unison. Carl stood up, and they wasted no time leaping into his arms, feeling the joy and excitement in their tight embrace. Over a year had passed since he last laid eyes on them. His cheeks were wet with tears, and try as he might, he couldn't stop them from falling.

"I love you, Daddy," they said over and over. "We missed you so much." Andrea stood at the doorway and watched with a smile on her face. After 10 minutes of hugging and talking with them, Andrea finally said. "Your Daddy and I need to talk. I'm going to take you back to the patio with Gramma and Grampa for lunch. We'll meet you in a few minutes."

Andrea took the two kids back to the patio and returned by herself. She sat on the chair opposite the desk. "Carl, the kids miss you terribly. I want to move here with them so you can see them every day. I've looked into private schools and they have many of them. They boast an excellent British school education, which is better than anything we have in Toronto."

Carl, still reeling from the emotional roller coaster of seeing his kids after such a long time, was at a loss for words. This was totally unexpected. He knew that one day he would re-connect with them, but it surprised him that Andrea would do this. *There must be something more to this. This is out if character for her.*

Andrea glanced at her hands, then at Carl. "I can see it in your eyes," she said, as if reading his thoughts. "You are wondering why I would disrupt their lives and move them to this place."

Andrea paused as if she had to collect her thoughts. "A few things have changed. Doctors diagnosed me with bipolar disorder, and I've started taking lithium, which has stabilized my mood swings. I am a different person now, Carl. Being able to think rationally and having emotional stability has helped me navigate through this terrible ordeal. I could never understand how you could go through life as if nothing was too big a problem, while small, trivial things would send me into an emotional spiral. I understand now that I was the one with the problem."

Carl listened intently. Andrea paused again. "How long have you had this condition?" asked Carl.

"I've had it for as long as I can remember," replied Andrea. "Remember Bali?"

"Bali was probably the most memorable and most exquisite time in my life. I had never experienced the feeling of being the greatest man in the world as I experienced during that month."

"I knew something was wrong with me when I was in university. Among my friends, there were a few who had been to Bali and could relate to my mood swings. They discovered the perceived benefits of micro-dosing Psilocybin and had an unforgettable experience. Like them, I also found that being in Bali cured me of my illness and brought me immense happiness. I truly meant every single word of those things I told you. It was only when I started experiencing severe side effects that I realized I needed to quit the psilocybin. Do you recall when I experienced excruciating cramps coupled with waves of diarrhea, nausea and relentless vomiting? Well, that was from the magic mushrooms. At that moment, I truly believed my life was about to end. I could see the worry in your eyes when you looked at me."

His brow furrowed in anxiety as he confessed, "I was very worried about you. I still remember the gripping fear of the thought of losing you, and the overwhelming dread that consumed me. It makes sense now; I mean about the mushrooms. The release of dopamine and serotonin in the brain caused by them creates a sense of wellbeing and happiness. Some experts believe that a decrease in dopamine receptors and a reduction in serotonin release, creating a chemical imbalance that causes the mood swings with bipolar disorder."

Andrea nodded in agreement. "Another thing I've learned is that individuals with bipolar disorder often attribute all their life difficulties to their partner. That is exactly what I did to you. Carl, I accept complete blame for this fiasco. It's entirely my doing. I am sincerely sorry. I am the one responsible for shattering your life into pieces." As a tear rolled down her cheek, her voice caught in her throat and she fell silent.

As Carl glanced at her, he felt she was truly remorseful. He looked at her with empathy and said, "Andrea, it's not your fault when someone deceives you, like Yursenko. The blame for the sexual assault charges lies with me, not with you. What fascinates me is finding my way through life's challenges, like navigating a maze. Although I have suffered a dramatic downfall, I still believe that I am in a better position than before. Even if I am completely exonerated, I cannot envision myself going back to a surgical practice. I feel so much more alive now. Life is full of unexpected surprises and unpredictable detours. To conquer all of them and still maintain a sense of self-worth, that is the valuable lesson I've learned. Each day, I discover new reasons to be thankful. Today, seeing Carl Junior and Simone made it a truly spectacular day. Talking with you right now helps me understand your struggles. These are the things that bring me immense gratitude."

Andrea looked at Carl incredulously as she dried her eyes. "Thank you for listening and being so understanding," she said. She turned to leave. When she got to the door, she turned back to look at Carl and asked, "How did you figure out the password on the USB stick?"

Carl smiled, his eyes twinkling with fond memories, and said, "Andrea, how could I ever forget that? The address that held all our cherished memories was 69 Heavenly Passion Path, our love sanctuary in Bali during that enchanting month. It took some effort to get the capitals right for the password to work, but eventually, I succeeded. I know it was a time filled with great happiness for you as well."

Chapter 33

Carl began typing. 'It was a dark and stormy night,' and then he stopped. He immediately had no idea what to write next. After much encouragement from Andy and Andrea, he agreed to write a book about his experiences and his newfound sense of self worth. The conversation he had a week ago with them prompted him to give it a try, but so far, he couldn't get the creative juices flowing.

"You were at the pinnacle of your profession, a prominent surgeon and president of the surgical society," said Andy. "When people saw you, their first thought was you had the perfect millionaire family of a beautiful wife, a smart son, and a cute but highly intelligent daughter. Then all that came crashing down. Before you knew it, you were living in a rooming house, getting the shit beat out of you by the dregs of society."

Carl laughed out loud, his laughter echoing across the outdoor patio. They were at their favorite spot in the Basilica restaurant, drinking beer after another successful week with fully booked charters. The sun was about to set and the sky had turned into a kaleidoscope of colours. The new clients had arrived earlier that afternoon and all seven completely full sailboats with their captains had set sail just before sunset to anchor off Jolly Harbour, excited to be going on their now famous Antigua circumnavigation adventure.

Carl remarked, "It just goes to show how appearances can be incredibly deceiving and how easily the thread of keeping everything together can fall apart. It was astonishing to me how rapidly this happens when someone wants to unravel that thread."

"Ha ha," said Andy. "That's one way of looking at it. What is more fascinating to me is how anyone can recover from such a fall. I've heard of resilience taking over and people climbing back after such a tumble, but I'm sure it is much more common to see the opposite. What prevented you from turning into one of those bearded and barefoot cases that we see at stop lights with a sign asking for money so you can buy food?"

Carl thought for a moment, unsure of how much to tell Andy, and then said, "The sheer shock of witnessing the unfolding of multiple terrible events left me paralyzed by anxiety, longing for nothing more than to sleep with the hope of never waking up. It was what Ray called 'free floating' anxiety. It incapacitated me to where my mind was perpetually clouded and I was living in a brain fog. I no longer cared what was going to happen to me, and I had convinced myself this was what I deserved."

Andy pointed his finger at Carl. "That is precisely the point I am trying to make. The moment you hit the rock bottom, the world around you seemed to come crashing down, leaving you feeling broken and lost. You had few remnants of your previous life, only fragments and fading memories. Everyone in the rooming house had experienced the same unfair treatment from a biased system, but you were the exception who managed to overcome it. How could such a thing happen?"

"Having a handful of people who had faith in me proved to be an advantage. Despite warnings from patrons, Bob Jones made the controversial decision to hire me, a registered sexual offender, to work at Tim Horton's. I have always remembered how you showed up at my trial. It meant a lot to me. I saw when you gave me the thumbs up sign. At first, I found it perplexing that while everyone else had distanced themselves from me, you remained a steadfast source of support. Memories of our past flooded my mind, reminding me of the unbreakable bond we shared. I knew then, as I always have, that I too would never abandon you."

"How is it you seem to harbour such little resentment for all those that ruined your life? It would be so easy to remain bitter and disappointed by those who brought you down. Stephanie, the CMPA lawyer, the District Attorney, the criminal lawyer, who wanted nothing to with you once you ran out of money, just to name a few. What about all those who simply ignored your plight? Your colleagues that ghosted you as though you never existed. Don't you feel angry about them?"

Carl scratched his beard. He had a fashionable short beard

that was turning into a salt and pepper colour. "You know, I quickly realized bitterness and anger consume so much energy. I found if I turned that energy into improving my life and looking for positive things to be grateful for, I was much happier. I...." Andrea and the kids interrupted his conversation by joining them.

"Daddy, Daddy," they shouted. After giving him a hug, they ran off to the adjacent beach to play in the sand and look for shells.

"I'm trying to convince Carl to write a book about what happened to him," said Andy.

Andrea sat in the empty seat beside them. She glanced at the enthusiastic gestures of Andy and laughed. "Maybe you should write the book for him?" she suggested.

"No way," said Andy. "It's essential that it's him, so others can understand his journey and realize that hope never disappears, regardless of the circumstances."

"Maybe you could relate your experiences with living the bipolar nightmare," suggested Andrea. "It's a secret that few are willing to divulge. Mental health problems are often stigmatized, leading most to choose silence as their coping mechanism. My bipolar condition fuelled your downfall in this case. This is something that fills me with deep regret. Had I effectively dealt with it, this chain of events could have been avoided. Consider the countless individuals enduring anguish as they witness their partners silently battling undiagnosed bipolar disorder. The partners are shouldering the blame for all their unhappiness, creating a sense of inadequacy and helplessness. You could vividly describe all these details in your book, having lived through it."

"It might be difficult for me to write about everything that happened for fear of exposing my vulnerability and weaknesses," replied Carl. "Besides, most people are uninterested in hearing the story of finding contentment with whatever comes their way. Instead, they prefer to chase after the elusive American dream of financial prosperity as a means to attain happiness."

"Try it anyway," said Andy. "Others may benefit from what you went through."

Carl reflected on that conversation with Andy and Andrea as he sat there now with complete writer's block after just the first sentence. He did not know how to create a story from events and images floating around in his mind. In an exasperated move, he deleted the only sentence he had written. After a few minutes, he began typing. 'My name is Carl Mackenzie. The story I am about to tell you is a true account of the events that led to my downfall and the resurrection of my life by searching for gratitude in everyday occurrences.'

Carl continued to write, 'The applause was thunderous. I looked at the 450 surgeons from across Ontario who had taken two days off from their busy schedule to come to my meeting. The conference hall went quiet as I.....'

Chapter 34

Carl's fingers danced across the keyboard as he typed with fervour on his computer. The sentences flowed from him like a rushing river, as if he couldn't type them fast enough. As the ideas flooded his mind, his fingers flew across the keys. He aimed for a captivating narrative, blurring the lines between fact and fiction, while also capturing his raw emotions in the moment.

After saying goodnight to the kids at Andrea's apartment, he found he made the most progress writing his book during the peacefulness of the night in his business office at Jolly Harbour. He looked up, his eyes strained from staring at the screen for the past hour. Just outside the door to the office, someone stood, their silhouette visible through the frosted glass.

With a loud bang, the door burst open, startling Carl. The Russian, accompanied by his three imposing bodyguards, entered the room. Carl's intense gaze locked with their piercing glare.

"Hello Carl," said the Russian. "I've come to finish off what I started."

As he stared at the hanging jowls and the tiny eyes embedded deeply in fat, Carl felt an overwhelming sense of calm. The lingering suspicion that the Russian would seek revenge had always loomed in the back of his mind, making this unexpected visit somewhat expected. Not a sound escaped Carl's lips as he maintained his silence. Based on the previous encounter, he understood the Russian was the one who wanted to be in charge of the show.

The news about the Russian had made headlines throughout the world. For a gigantic man, he had remained surprisingly elusive to capture. The rumours had him placed in Syria, where he could conduct his illegal business without fear of capture. Others believed he had a mansion in the war-torn country of the Ukraine. Authorities there had their hands full managing the war against the invading militia and had little resources to deal with criminal elements like the Russian. For now, he remained free to roam the planet.

"They confiscated my boat, $300 million worth of luxury now gone, thanks to you," he continued. "That, along with the $100 million you stole from me, makes me the laughingstock of my peers. You see, I need to redeem my status as the man in charge. That is why I need to make an example out of you."

Carl simply stared at him. He knew nothing he said or did would make any difference now. The Russian seemed hellbent on finishing him. "Boys, tie him up!"

The burly bodyguards trussed his hands together with zip ties, then moved on to his feet. They were both tightly bound to the chair with zip ties, unable to move an inch. They forcefully silenced him by stuffing a gag into his mouth. Underneath his chair, they positioned a box measuring approximately 6 inches wide. Wires connected it to an electric timer that they would trigger to go off after 5 minutes.

"You have 5 minutes to regret your decision to send the bitcoin back to Canada instead of to me before you get blown to pieces." He turned to leave the office as the timer ticked down to 4:30 minutes. "Oh, by the way," he sneered, "The other explosions you will hear just before you turn to cinders are your precious boats getting blown up. I wanted to ensure that I filled your last moments with nothing but misery."

He and his team of bodyguards turned and left. Carl glanced at the timer, its red digits counting down the seconds. There were only 3:30 minutes remaining. He attempted to shift in the chair, but he could only squirm uncomfortably. As he sat there helplessly, a deafening noise erupted from the marina, followed by a brilliant orange flash and the sight of flames engulfing the docks where his beloved boats were moored. The clock flashed 2:30. He could see people rushing to the docks in confused panic. 1:30 minutes remained. Carl needed to do something, and quickly. He wiggled his toes; they touched the floor. 30 seconds left. He wiggled his toes more.

Then a loud explosion followed by silence.

Chapter 35

Confusion clouded his mind when he opened his eyes. The surroundings were unfamiliar, as was the bed in which he was lying. A woman wearing white came to his bed. He could see her mouth moving, but could hear nothing. She started shouting and he could catch a few words. "Your eardrums have ruptured, so you will have trouble hearing until they heal." Carl nodded.

"No one can believe you are alive after the explosion! Are you hurt anywhere?" Carl shook his head.

He remembered the last moments just before the explosion. He wiggled his toes on the floor, providing him with just enough to roll the chair towards the glass door. This momentum, along with the force from the explosion, propelled him almost harmlessly through the glass onto the grass in front of the office, where he lost consciousness from the impact.

Another man walked into his room. The name tag said 'Bogdan Boyko, General Surgeon'. He sat on the edge of the bed. Bogdan had a deep voice, which made it easier for Carl to hear him. "I believe you've suffered a mild concussion from the explosion, but fortunately, there don't seem to be any other injuries. We did a total body CT scan, which allowed for a comprehensive view of the internal structures throughout the body. There are no signs of damage or breakage."

Carl eyed his name tag suspiciously. "Your name, is it Russian?"

Bogdan shook his head and laughed. "Far from it! The Russians would have destroyed me if I had let them. The police told me they found you unconscious. They mentioned something about an explosion but were sketchy on the details. Tell me what happened."

Carl told him the story. After Carl finished speaking, Bogdan leaned back and said, "I have heard about the Russian. His true name remains a mystery, known only to himself. He moves silently through the murky shadows of the underworld. His villa, located just outside of Kiev in the Ukraine, is a grand and opulent residence. My familiarity with these details stems from my experience as a surgeon from the Ukraine. I fled when the war with Russia erupted, fearing for the safety of my wife, who is Russian. The Ukrainian resistance fighters would have taken her life. My Ukrainian degrees left me with limited options, forcing me to settle for this desolate island. My brother is also a General Surgeon in Kiev. We were in practice together and had the largest laparoscopic practice in the country."

Carl replied, "I used to work as a General Surgeon in Canada, but now I have this chartering company which the Russian wanted to destroy. When he finds out I am still alive, he will come after me again."

Bogdan had a stern expression on his face. "There is no doubt about that. He supplies arms and weapons to the Ukraine, but also sells them to North Korea at inflated prices. North Korea sells them back to Russia and uses them to attack the Ukraine. He has been the dominant force behind all the ransomware attacks in the US and Canada, yet no one has the courage to stand up to him. He is vengeful and vindictive."

Andrea and Andy knocked at the door. "Carl," they shouted together, "No one can believe you are alive!" They rushed over and hugged him.

"What is the condition of the boats? How much damage did they sustain?" asked Carl after they settled into the chairs that were in the room.

Andy sighed out deeply before he replied. "*ILEANA* burned and sank when they towed her out to sea to prevent other boats from catching on fire. The other catamarans were undamaged. I removed the C4 explosives that they plastered to their hulls. A heat sensitive triggering device attached the explosives together, but because the marina staff contained the fire on the docks so quickly, the devices never activated."

Carl pondered these thoughts for a moment before uttering, "The Russian will relentlessly pursue me once more. I need to stop him before he causes any more damage. The thought of the next time involving both of you fills me with dread, and I won't allow it to happen. I have a plan."

Carl detailed his plan to both Andrea and Andy, explaining how each of their roles would be crucial for the plan to work. Carl turned to Bogdan and said. "Your role in the plan is key, as is your brother's. Are you OK with that?"

Bogdan smiled and nodded his head.

"We need to find a way to do this, leaving no trace behind," said Carl. "Otherwise, we'll be living in hiding forever."

****

Within 24 hours, Carl and Andy were on a plane heading for Warsaw. They had flown to New York City, then connected on a flight to Warsaw, Poland.

"How are you feeling?" asked Carl.

"Considering what you did to me, I feel pretty good," replied Andy.

"Well, Andrea found us a ride with her cousin Beata, from the Underground Ukrainian Movement in Poland," replied Carl. "I met her a few years ago when she came to visit us in Toronto. She'll drive us across the border and right to the private hospital where Borys Boyko, Bogdan's brother, works. From there, we'll unroll the rest of the plan."

Customs and immigration authorities summoned Andy as soon as he landed in Warsaw. Carl's heart raced as he anxiously watched the officials escort Andy into a separate room. They ushered Carl through the customs and immigration area, guiding him towards the arrival lounge where he could wait. Carl waited impatiently in the room, his footsteps echoing as he paced back and forth. He texted his ride to tell her there was a delay. Carl was worried. After 2 hours, Andy appeared with a smile on his face.

"Something triggered the alarms as we walked through them," said Andy. "They made me strip and they searched me. They finally let me go and they couldn't find anything. I think we are good to go!"

A text message from Carl summoned the driver, who arrived to collect them at the curb. Beata brought her 2024 Volkswagen Trendline to a complete stop. Her long dark hair, which was stylishly tied in a ponytail at the back, strikingly highlighted by her dark brown eyes. She appeared exactly as Carl remembered her from her past visit to Toronto, unchanged by time. With a self-assured smile that radiated confidence, she communicated a clear message of unwavering trust and steadfast commitment. "The drive to Kiev is a long one, a full 10 hours, but the quiet hum of the vehicle's engine and subtle vibrations of the car should lull you into a comfortable sleep. You can fold down the seats in the back, providing a comfortable sleeping space. We filled the cooler to the brim with refreshing drinks and delicious sandwiches. In just 3 hours, we'll be crossing the border into Ukraine. With enough spare gasoline to make it back to Warsaw, we only need to stop for quick bathroom breaks."

Carl and Andy crawled into the back seat and fell asleep within a few minutes.

Chapter 36

At first, it surprised Carl that Andy would agree. This was something that would push the boundaries of their friendship. It was one thing to offer to help, but to agree to this seemed a little crazy, even to Carl. Carl knew he would have done the same thing for Andy without questioning the wisdom of the plan, so intuitively, it made sense that Andy would do the same for him. Still, Andy had been through so much grief already because of Carl. His precious *ILEANA* burned and sank with the Russian's retaliation. A sensible response would have been for Andy and Carl to leave the Russian's fate to the professionals. Their plan was full of holes, and there were gaping weaknesses that could cause it to fail.

"Look," said Andy. "This situation requires drastic measures. I agree it is risky, and I could get blown to kingdom come, but if we don't think outside the box, the Russian will track you down and kill you. He has already demonstrated his ability to evade the authorities. We know he will continue to do so. We have to take matters into our own hands, otherwise all of us will now suffer. I am sure he will target me as well now. He knows how close we are."

"It would not offend me if you said 'no' to this," replied Carl. "There is no guarantee it will work out. There could be complications from the surgery. The C4 could detonate prematurely, splaying your guts across the Ukraine."

"Enough talk," said Andy. "Let's do this! I've made up my mind."

The anesthesiologist put Andy asleep and Carl had performed the first surgery 12 hours prior to leaving Antigua. Bogdan had assisted with the procedure.

****

Carl opened the small incision under the umbilicus, the same one he had used two days ago. He slid in a 10 mm port into the abdomen. He inserted the 5 mm ports after insufflating the abdomen with five liters of carbon dioxide. A clear image of the distended stomach, which contained the plastic bag he had inserted two days ago, appeared. He cut the long staple line to open the stomach wide enough to remove the large plastic package that filled the stomach. He opened the previous incision just above the bladder. The deeper sutures he cut with scissors to open the small incision. Using a plastic wound protector to prevent a wound infection, he pulled the sealed plastic bag that had been in the stomach to just below the incision. Using surgical instruments, he opened the plastic bag. One by one, he removed the contents from the plastic bag and placed them on the surgical table. When the bag was empty, he removed it from the abdomen. He changed his surgical gloves and closed the muscle layer with sutures and the skin with staples.

The next step involved re-insufflating the abdomen with

carbon dioxide. He placed the laparoscope in the umbilical port and watched the image on the monitor. Using 3 firings of the stapler, he closed the stomach securely. After inspecting the staple line for bleeding and suctioning the small amount of fluid, he removed the laparoscope and the ports and closed the skin incisions with the skin stapler. He applied the dressings and Carl transported Andy to the recovery room.

"You performed that operation nicely, Carl," said Borys, smiling in the recovery room. "Since the war, no one asks questions when unusual operations are done. We operate on a lot of civilian and soldier casualties, but tonight there were none, so we had the operating room to ourselves. What will you do now?"

"Now I have the C4 and detonators, I will finish what I came for. Your brother told me he was a demolition specialist in the Ukrainian army before he became a surgeon. He gave me a quick course in demolition before I implanted the explosives into Andy. I feel confident I can set the explosives and detonate them without harming myself. By the time Andy is awake, I'll be back to pick him up for the drive back to Warsaw."

"Good luck then!" said Borys.

With the explosives and detonator safely stowed in his carry-on backpack, Carl walked out of the hospital. In the hospital parking lot, Beata, his driver, patiently awaited his arrival. Carl's phone rang, filling the car with its shrill, piercing sound. It was Andrea.

"I have some more information about the villa.," she explained. "I successfully infiltrated the Russian's security system, disabling the sensors that guard the entrance to the underground tunnel. I learned about the security systems used by these criminals when I discovered they used my software in the cyberattack. The system I hacked was a similar system when I retrieved the $100 million and put it on my USB. The Russian uses the same security software for his villa. Since they have never used the tunnel, I am hopeful it hasn't collapsed after the passage of five years since its excavation. According to the building plans, a small shed can be found approximately 500 meters away from the villa. It is in the northwest corner of a farmer's field. Hidden beneath a wooden table, you will find a small hatch that leads to an underground tunnel. Follow that tunnel to the end. You will come to a locked door. Place the explosives in the ceiling above immediately above the door. The Russian's arsenal of rockets and weapons are directly above. The explosion should cause them to ignite, blowing the villa to kingdom come."

Carl took a mental note of the instructions and instructed the driver to take him to the GPS coordinates Andrea had given him the day before. The villa was brightly lit, with indirect lighting coming in from all directions. A wrought-iron fence 10 feet high surrounded the villa. As they drove by, Carl could see armed guards with their dogs walking on the property. Beata pulled up to the small shed Andrea had described.

"Wait here," Carl instructed Beata. Carl walked over to the shed and carefully opened the door, checking to be certain no one was around. The wooden table was heavy, but Carl pushed it to one side with his shoulder to expose the hatch. He checked around the edges to be certain he could see no wires which might indicate a bobby trap but saw none. Carl lifted the hatch and turned on his headlamp. A musky smell of damp earth filled his nostrils as he descended into the tunnel.

The tunnel was about 6 feet high and 3 feet wide. Wooden struts along its length prevented the tunnel from collapsing. Wooden planks lined the floor, and he easily trudged along the tunnel, ducking occasionally when a loose strut from the ceiling blocked his way. The smell was of damp earth and mildew. A few brown puddles appeared on the pathway and he avoided them. It seemed clear to Carl, no one had used this walkway for some time. No imprints of footsteps appeared in the areas where the soft mud appeared. Some spider webs lined the ceiling, and he brushed them away.

After walking for 10 minutes, he came to a locked door. He opened his backpack and removed the plastic explosives. The ceiling strut was loose above the doorway, and he stuffed the 10 lbs of C4 explosives into the defect and jammed the wooden strut to keep the explosives in place. The detonator he attached with the wire. Andrea had instructed him to feed as much of the antenna wire through the crack in the doorway as high as possible so it would receive the signal to detonate from the remote when Carl was safely out of the tunnel.

Carl hastily made his way back down the tunnel, trying to regain his bearings. As he climbed up the ladder, the rusty rungs creaked under his weight. He switched off his headlamp, plunging himself into darkness. Slowly, he replaced the table over the cover and cautiously opened the door, revealing the sound of crickets chirping in the night. The Volkswagen sat silently on the road, blending in with the darkness as its lights remained off. Beata gestured enthusiastically from behind the wheel, urging him to climb in.

"Drive by the front gate of the villa slowly. I need to detonate the explosives," said Carl. Beata put the Volkswagen into gear and to the front gate. Carl pressed the remote. Nothing happened.

"I need you to drive by again. This time, get close to the edge of the road, so we are as close to the building as possible."

Beata turned the car around, and they drove by again, catching another glimpse of the brightly lit mansion. Carl pressed the remote. Once again, there was complete silence and stillness.

"Stop the car!" Carl shouted urgently, his voice filled with panic. Reaching into his backpack, he retrieved a roll of duct tape and tightly wrapped it around the remote. By this time, a guard had become suspicious and leaned in closer to peer through the ornate wrought-iron gate at the Volkswagen.

As soon as the car stopped, Carl leaped out and dashed towards the fence. With a swift motion, he cocked his arm back and hurled the remote into the yard, watching it soar through the air before landing about 20 feet from the house. The guard's voice boomed in Ukrainian, catching the attention of another guard, who promptly appeared. He gripped his assault rifle, his finger hovering over the trigger, as if prepared to shoot at Carl.

Then, suddenly, there was an explosion. The ground rumbled ominously, causing the entire villa to shake as it lifted three feet into the air, before the deafening blast finally echoed through the air. The blast sent the two guards soaring through the air before plummeting to the ground, lying motionless. Carl swiftly retreated, his heart pounding, and jumped into the car. When Carl turned around, the mesmerizing sight of the sky transforming into a vibrant shade of orange filled the horizon. The flames leapt into the sky, reaching a height of at least 100 feet.

As Beata sped away, the last image burned into Carl's mind. Looking through the rear windshield, was the sight of the collapsed villa reduced to a pile of burning rubble.

Chapter 37

After completing the last chapter of his book, Carl eagerly sent the manuscript to Jenet Garner, an editor based in Vancouver. Jenet meticulously revised the story, enhancing the reading experience and rectified any grammatical mistakes. Carl's editor provided a wealth of excellent recommendations, all of which he gladly accepted and incorporated into his project.

"I heard about the destruction of the villa on the news," said Jenet when she called Carl to discuss the manuscript. "The CNN story detailed the aftermath of a devastating drone strike, ordered by Putin, that left the villa in ruins. The news reported was that they unknowingly wiped out a key weapons provider. Putin adamantly denied that it was their actions that targeted the villa. Yet, the version you present in your narrative contradicts the news story account."

Carl listened intently as Jenet reviewed her comments. "You have to decide whether this story of yours is in fact an accurate account of what happened, or a work of fiction," she said.

In the book, Carl deliberately withheld a couple of crucial pieces of information. With her hacking skills, Andrea gained access to the video security system and could verify that the Russian was indeed inside the villa. She stumbled across him when he visited the massive walk-in fridge. In disbelief, she watched him devour an astonishing amount of food stored there in record time. She witnessed him attacking a roasted chicken, tearing off the wings and legs while using two hands to stuff them into his mouth. Only a few of the larger bones remained from the chicken. The smaller bones along with the skin, he swallowed whole. A few of the guards lounged around the kitchen and manned the security station, but no one else was in the villa.

"I would prefer to let the reader decide what they wish to believe," replied Carl. "The part about sneaking C4 explosives inside a plastic bag, which I carefully inserted into Andy's stomach using laparoscopic techniques before we departed from Antigua, feels incredibly implausible, doesn't it? I thought they had caught us at the polish customs in Warsaw, but the officers quickly noticed the recent surgery, visible through the surgical clips. It was clear to me they suspected the surgical clips had triggered the sensors when we walked through them."

"Yes, that transportation of explosives sounds implausible, but this is your story. I watched an hour-long program about the Russian," said Jenet. "No one knew his name. He was involved in every illegal activity you could think of, including the spectacular cyber attacks that occurred in Ontario. Since the destruction of the villa and anyone inside, the cyber attacks across North America have come to a halt. He did not seem like a very nice person."

"And don't forget about his vindictiveness," said Carl. "He blew me out of the front door of my office in retaliation for sending back the bitcoin to the Ministry of Health."

Jenet paused for a moment. "Yeah. Perhaps you should worry. Considering your past experiences with him, aren't you afraid of facing further retaliation? What if he wasn't in the villa when it exploded?"

Carl chuckled because he knew the Russian was there that night, and others had confirmed his presence in the villa. "The Ukrainian special forces said he was there at the time of explosion, and that is the most accurate information we have on him. I think I have nothing to worry about."

"OK," said Jenet. "Let me check my notes." Carl heard the rustling of paper. "Oh, here it is. Bali was a symphony of sensations for you - the melodic sounds of traditional music, the tantalizing aroma of street food, and the warm, tropical breeze against your skin, but best of all was the extraordinary sexual adventure with a woman who had self medicated herself to the point where she had overdosed. Do you have concerns about inadvertently supporting the use of micro dosing psilocybin as a viable treatment for bipolar disorder? In multiple instances, you described it as one of the most extraordinary sexual experiences of your life, spending a month with a woman who was perpetually stoned on the stuff."

Carl thought about his answer. "It came as a surprise when Andrea confessed she had been taking magic mushrooms in Bali, a secret she had kept until now. From my perspective, I thought this was the kind of love that made your heart flutter and your palms sweat when you have found the right woman. The point I wanted to convey was that I wasted my remaining time with her chasing after a nonexistent illusion, the one etched in my brain from my time with her in Bali. In a regular relationship, that fiery intensity might still arise, but not with such unwavering fervour for an entire month."

"Ah ah," said Jenet. "Makes sense. I still find it unbelievable you could rise from the bottom to resurrect yourself as a new identity, using gratitude as the lever. I think you could explain that part better."

"Using words to explain how gratitude works is a challenge," Carl replied. "It's all about the way it stirs up different feelings inside of you. What's fascinating is that those in your vicinity can sense the energy you emit, and the impact intensifies with each occurrence."

"Huh," said Jenet. "That's all the comments I have for now, then. Good luck with the sales."

****

Surpassing Carl's expectations by a wide margin, the book sold over 1 million copies in less than six months, delighting him.

Carl poured some of the money into their charter business, hoping to see it flourish. He set aside a portion of the money in trust to provide financial support for Andrea and the children. With his new schedule, Carl had ample time to bond with Carl Junior and Simone, something he never had the opportunity to do during his time as a surgeon. This was the best time of his life, second only to the unforgettable Bali experience.

After walking the kids to school one day, he felt an eerie sensation creeping down his neck, as if someone were observing his every move. He spun around, feeling the wind whip through his hair. On the balcony of a condominium, at the top of the hill, a man stood with binoculars, focused directly on him. The scared face, disfigured and twisted, was an ugly mess, impossible for Carl to ignore. What gave him away was his tremendous obesity, with abdominal rolls of fat hanging to his knees. The watchful gaze of the Russian never wavered as Carl stared directly at him, making it clear that he was under constant surveillance.

The End